Sterling
BRIDGE

Sterling BRIDGE

CHAD ROBERT PARKER

BONNEVILLE
BOOKS
An imprint of Cedar Fort, Inc.
Springville, Utah

Photo on page 135 courtesy of Judd Parker
Photo on back cover courtesy of
Special Collections & Archives
Merrill-Cazier Library
Utah State University

ISBN 13: 978-1-4621-1735-2

Published by Bonneville Books, an imprint of Cedar Fort, Inc.
2373 W. 700 S., Springville, UT 84663
Distributed by Cedar Fort, Inc. www.cedarfort.com

LIBRARY OF CONGRESS CATALOGING-IN-PUBLICATION DATA

Parker, Chad Robert, 1978-
Sterling Bridge / Chad Robert Parker.
pages cm
ISBN 978-1-4621-1735-2 (perfect : alk. paper)
1. Mormons--Fiction. 2. Catholics--Fiction. 3. Country life--Utah--Fiction. 4. Domestic fiction. I. Title.
PS3616.A74425S84 2015
813'.6--dc23

2015011908

Cover design by Michelle May
Cover design © 2015 by Lyle Mortimer
Edited and typeset by Justin Greer

Printed in the United States of America

10 9 8 7 6 5 4 3 2 1

Printed on acid-free paper

In memory of one of Tooele County's
best-known citizens,
Sterling Richard Harris
(1899–1992)

Contents

1
Schools of Thought

I was twelve years old when I chose Sterling Harris as my role model and hero. He has remained as such throughout my life. Today we reflect on his great life." I cast my eyes from the pulpit to the closed casket before me and then around a diverse solemn assembly that filled the chapel, all dressed respectfully in their best Sunday attire, looking on with love. I marveled at them all united together as one. It wasn't always that way. It choked me up and, as I paused, all of the memories rushed back.

CЗ

Our rooster's shrill morning call jolted me awake to the reality of 1926. I squinted at a timepiece set off the side of my bed, grabbed it, and blinked through sunrays let in by wooden shutters.

I tucked my head underneath my afghan, my hand still hanging from the bed holding the time—6:10 a.m. Holes of light permeated through the woven yarns, illuminating patches of my face. In disgust, I slid the handheld clock across the dark, dirt-worn wood floor far away from me; it scraped loudly to a stop. I rolled over, shielding myself from the window's sunlight and then dug for sheets clinging at my waist; these I pulled over my head.

"Joe," Mother's voice called sharply from outside the bedroom door. "Get up! You need to be hoofing it by seven o'clock. I don't want you riding the train!" The door creaked open slightly. I rubbed open one eye, momentarily, but she hadn't entered. With my nose exposed, I breathed deeply. "Breakfast," I mumbled, staring gloomily at the bedroom door and stretching my arms. Then I stared up at the ceiling, looked back at the door, and buried my nose and eyes underneath the safety of my down pillow. I dozed off.

Firm, warm hands squeezed my cold toes free of their covering. I squirmed and kicked, but the grip remained. I rubbed my eyes and looked at the easy grin of my father. "Good morning, bright eyes," he said. "It's a beautiful day!" He tossed my timepiece onto the bed next to me.

I moaned and looked away. "Maybe for you. Do I really have to go to school there? None of the other outsiders do." I stared at the wall beyond him.

Dad put a hand on my shoulder. "Come now, you don't want to be late for your first day. Blend in. Make some friends. It will all work out. You'll see!" My parents figured the younger the better, considering grades six through twelve were combined in the establishment of Tooele. The idea was that maybe the other students might not notice if I started school a few years before I really had no choice, but I knew better. No outsider would go unnoticed in Oldtown.

I bolted upright. "Why me? You never had to!" I jumped to the floor, walked to the window, and stared out at our front yard—a gas station. My countenance softened. "Dad, who's that?"

Dad walked to the window and gasped. "That there, son, is our first customer. I'll see you outside." Dad excitedly ruffled my hair and then left with an upbeat pace.

I buttoned up a shirt over my long underwear and stepped into a pair of trousers, pulling suspenders up over my shoulders, and threw on my felt cap. I walked downstairs, leaned up against the entry of the kitchen, and smiled as I observed Mom humming a tune and twirling through a few dance steps in between flipping eggs with a spatula in a worn-out pan over the propane stove.

Mom always said she won Dad with her cooking, not with her dancing. When she was seventeen her mom had died, and she learned how to handle all of the household chores. I knew she wished she could go dancing with my dad someday.

She abruptly stopped two-stepping upon seeing me. "I had to reheat your food."

"Sorry," I muttered.

"If you were more like your father, you would never be late for a meal."

"I wish I were!" I proclaimed. "Then I could be like everyone else in Newtown." The chair screeched as I sat up to the table.

"Don't say that. And don't you dare wake up the other kids." Mom set a plate of food in front of me. "You know we just want a better life for you and your siblings than your Dad had."

I passively pushed the food around my plate with a fork.

"You better eat. You're going to be on time whether you've eaten or not."

Slowly, I took one bite and swished it from cheek to cheek in my mouth.

A car horn honked a few blows, as if it were amusing to the driver.

Mom and I exchanged curious looks. She shrugged and then set the dish towel and the pan she was drying aside. I followed her out the front door.

"Now if only I can get the football position, then I can afford it." The man guffawed.

"This is my wife, Jenny, and my son, Joe." Dad leaned on our newly installed Texaco gasoline pump. "Come meet this guy. He's a bigger dreamer than I am. He claims everyone in Oldtown will want to buy gas here once he tells them about it." Dad laughed.

"Well, can't pass up on free marketing. Mister, you must not be from around here." Mom stood bewildered. "Do you have friends in Tooele?"

"I'm here to make friends. My name is Sterling Harris." Sterling had been leaning against his standard black car. He walked over to shake our hands. Sterling was a stocky man in his early thirties. With a confident, stern, but cordial gaze he looked me over. "I'll be teaching at the high school. I hear it's your first day too. Care for a ride?"

I looked at Dad and then at Mom, not sure how I should answer.

"Thanks, sir, but we won't let Joe keep you. You've surely got preparations before class and he still has to eat his breakfast." Mom stood behind me, hands on my shoulders.

"I can wait," Sterling offered. "It's no bother, really."

"If he has to walk, then he'll be late," Dad warned Mom.

"So I'm old enough for school in Oldtown, but not to ride the cow catcher?" I shook my head and stomped off, slamming the front door behind me, surprising even myself.

Mom entered shortly after. "Joe Lacey, that was extremely rude! I want you to apologize to him."

I scowled and shoveled cold eggs and ham into my mouth. Then I sat defiantly still.

The car engine started up and the sound of the car pulled off into the distance.

"I'm disappointed in you." Mom walked out of the kitchen without saying anything more.

I braced my head with a clenched fist. Hollow pounding sounded against the outer wall, shaking the house. "What is that?" I asked.

Mom didn't answer.

I quickly ate the last several bites, scraping the metallic plate clean. I cleared it from the table into the sink, went into the living and gave Mom a kiss on her cheek, from which she pulled away, and then I rushed out the back door.

The sound of metal pounding on wood siding reverberated in the air. I stumbled down the large wooden steps on the outside of our home. Me clambering down the stairs caught Dad's attention. He stepped back away from his hammering and slipped the hammer into the loop of his pants along his thigh. With his thumbs tucked just inside the breast portion of his greasy coveralls, he rose up on his heels, pulled his coveralls forward, away from his body, and then rocked forward and rose onto his toes, tilting his head toward his creation approvingly.

I read out loud from a new sign nailed onto the garage portion of our home: *Watch the fat man go into the car.* I laughed, loudly. "I was wondering what all that racket was about." My teenage morning voice cracked. He didn't acknowledge my wisecrack, taking more time to admire the moment. I went and stood next to him to pay more homage. "Don't you think you should put a full service sign up?" He kept grinning.

As far as Dad was concerned, this was the next best thing to retirement. Really, he wanted nothing more than to be that fat man who owned a car, but for now the sign alone would do. Dad was among the first of the outsiders who came to Tooele from Anaconda, Montana, in 1912. Other Gentiles followed from Telluride, Colorado. Now only the stains of Father's clothing revealed his hand in helping form the Anaconda Copper Company that merged into the International Smelter. Mormon folk didn't much like a government operation taking over large swaths of land in their pioneering community, but then no one asked their opinion anyway. Desperate times had also forced people from all over Europe to find work wherever it was to be found and under whatever circumstances.

Dad proudly placed one hand on his hip as he continued to eye his new business and the other clutched the hammer at his leg.

"It looks good, Dad," I said.

"Doesn't it, though?" my father said.

"Are you still out there Peter Joseph Lacey, Junior? I better not hear that you were late on the first day!" Mom yelled from within the house. Dad and I both straightened up like deer sensing a hunter and then looked at one another and snickered.

I answered her back. "Just talking to Dad. He wanted to show me something."

Dad shot me a wide-eyed look of disbelief, as though I were crazy. His forehead glistened with perspiration in the morning sun; he casually pulled a hanky from his pocket and wiped the wrinkles smooth. While I stood composing myself, expelling a final giggle, he flicked his wrist and snapped the hanky into my hind parts.

"You tryin' to get us both in trouble?" he joked. I hopped away, covering my backside with my hands to avoid further cracks of punishment. Dad pulled a couple dollars from his pocket. "Hey, get your mom that record for her birthday." He smiled and waved me off with a yell. "Keep that pace, boy—I don't wanna hear it from your ma."

I trudged my way along a heavily trodden path, up alongside the Smelter worker's community housing project of evenly placed square plots of land, sectioned off by the federal government—homes for Yugoslavs, Slovenes, Croatians, Italians, Serbs, Bosnians, Greeks, Herzegovinians, Dalmatians, and Montenegros, among others. Many such neighboring countries were still at war with each other, but here in America the different nationalities were to get along as neighbors and coworkers, thrown together into the great melting pot. A grade school was also set up in Plat C for all of us foreigners. I stopped and stared longingly at my former school, somewhat in a daze. Most boys my age waited until the ninth grade before they even considered attending school in Oldtown; and they wouldn't have even considered it then, but school in Newtown only went through the eighth grade. Truth is, most dropped out of school entirely by then. This was to be the beginning of my sixth-grade year.

Closing my eyes and shaking my head, I freed myself from my paralyzed stance and refocused my gaze in a new direction. The white salty desert stretched before my view. I strode from the shade of one cottonwood tree to the next, all of them planted in a row. My head hung low as I walked. I took a deep breath and exhaled slowly. Then I continued plodding along until I crossed Vine Street, the access road between two different worlds. I looked each way. To the right I saw the plumes of smoke in front of the Oquirrh Mountains, where the smelter stood. To the left was Oldtown in the valley below me. The smelter was exactly four miles northeast of the Oldtown.

I breathed in deeply again and then sighed out loud. I continued to the railroad tracks. Next to the Tooele Valley Railway Depot were a dozen or so boys playing pass ball on a narrow patch of dirt between some tracks. I ducked out of view and sneaked past the final faded black boxcar—labeled Utah Coal Route in yellow lettering—to the front of the locomotive.

"Hey, Joe," a voice called out from behind me. "Where you goin'?" I stood with one hand on the train's engine and looked back over my shoulder. Mike Rinaldi stared up at me with furrowed brows.

"Ma needs something from Oldtown." I didn't want to tell this half-lie to a good friend, but it was just easier. Mike cocked his head and stared at me disbelievingly.

"See you at school, then, later?" Mike questioned. I shrugged.

I climbed up onto the cowcatcher at the very front of the locomotive. Above the triangular guard fencing was a platform where two or three people could sit comfortably. Successive clouds of smoke—larger in size with each burst—billowed into the air. With a few chugs and clangs, the train slowly moved forward. I braced myself as railroad cars consecutively pulled tight into place, creating a thunderous roll of rattling metal. I glanced hesitantly around the locomotive engine at the boys playing. With one pointing finger held in front of my squinting eye, I counted: ". . . ten, eleven. Missing one!" I whispered to myself. Then I stared down the track ahead, back toward home, and then at my feet as I shook my head, disgruntled. The locomotive lurched forward. The resulting gush of wind against my forehead blew my shabby gray cap off onto the ground. It was rolling away like a tumbleweed in the opposite direction. I jumped down and staggered to a stop, kicking up a lot of dust. Then I bounded after my cap. I pounced on it, got to my feet, and slapped the cap on my right leg to free it of dust, and then firmly fit it back on my head. The train was slowly picking up speed, but I definitely could have caught up to it had I wanted to. Instead, I ran toward the eleven boys as they continued pushing on each other in what probably looked more like a rugby scrum to an onlooker than any other form of football. The thirty-second freight cart passed with the caboose in tow.

"Is that Joe Lacey over there?" Across the tracks now open to all of the boy's view stood the austere man with the car, his hands cupped to his mouth to yell. His broad shoulders and bold stance made him look larger than life.

I did an about-face. The other boys finished tackling each other into a pile.

"You know that guy?" Mike stood next to me. "What does he want with you?"

Sterling beckoned with a big swinging motion of his arm. But when I made no motion toward him, he then approached us, confidently crossing the tracks.

"I'll be back." I scurried toward him.

"Hey Joe, you gonna introduce me to your friends?" Sterling walked right by me.

"You're not going to tell my parents, are you?" I held my hands out.

"What's to tell? I can still give you that ride to school." Sterling looked at his car.

"My friends don't know I'm switching schools." I spoke so only he would hear.

Sterling pivoted. With his back to my friends, he offered me a deal. "If you win, you'll never hear from me again, but if I win, you have to at least let me take you to school."

Now I felt calm and casually strode over to huddle up, certain I would never lose our bet.

"What's going on, Joe?" Mike asked.

"Oh, nothing! That old business man over there thinks he can show us a thing or two about pass ball." I pointed to Sterling, who was already lined up for a play, testing out his shiny boots in the dirt and pulling his slacks up away from his knees. "He says he'll get by me and sack the quarterback. If he fails, he will leave us alone." I spit in the dirt.

"And if you lose?" Jim Rinaldi joked.

"He can't catch up with you." I slugged Jim in the arm. "So don't let him!"

We lined up. Sterling had a similar stance to ours—one foot in front of the other—only he had his hands up, like he was ready to wrestle. The ball was snapped. He burst forward: first off the line. I braced for impact, wincing, but once he stutter-stepped me off-balance to the outside, he zipped through to the inside of me, untouched. Jim didn't even think to throw the ball away. His receiver brother, Joe Rinaldi, hadn't even turned his head around. Sterling pulled Jim gently enough to the ground. Sterling looked to me as if to say "we had a deal." We walked away. Behind me, I could hear the boys talking.

"What just happened?" Mike Rinaldi asked.

"Wow, did you see that?" Jim said. "What was that all about, anyway?"

"Yeah, what was that?" Mike quipped. "No one ever gets a hand on you usually."

I heard the football hit the ground. "So I let him, is all!" Jim must have spiked it.

"Sure you did!" Mike laughed.

"Huddle up! We've got a little more time before the nuns crack out the ruler." Jim sounded like he was all business again.

Sterling opened the passenger door and I hopped up onto the buckboard seat.

Sterling closed the door behind me and walked around to the driver's side. The car started smoothly and coasted through a couple shifts of gears. "Hold onto your cap! It might get a little bumpy." Sterling drove off the road, straight across the desert plain.

"Are you crazy? What are you doing?" I braced my hands on the dashboard.

"Making up time!" Sterling smiled. He drove the car on a direct path through sandy plains to connect up with Main Street, as if racing to catch the train.

I smiled as we bounced over a rock. "It would have been safer on the train."

"So why don't any of you boys play for the high school football team?"

"Are you kidding?" I took in his serious expression, coupled with his silence to mean that he wasn't. "I'm still in junior high. But I'll be lucky just to blend in before I reach high school—even with my ma being a native of Oldtown." I emphasized every point, speaking over the wind rushing in the window.

"Really? You look like a high schooler. How much do you weigh? Like 135?"

"How did you guess that?" I mused.

"From my days in the circus." Sterling grinned at my reaction. "I'm just pulling your leg. You weigh what I did when I started high school. That's a good size for your age. You know I'm also an outsider, not from around here. Should I be worried about that?" Sterling plowed the car through a bulrush bush.

"Well, at least you're Mormon, aren't you?"

"Yes," Sterling nodded. "So you're saying you need to be Mormon to go to public school now?" Sterling looked over at me, but I quickly looked out the window. "Doesn't it help that your Mom is a member?"

"Doesn't seem to. Not with how pa isn't a member. We sit alone. I go to sacrament meeting with ma, but no one is really a friend to us there," I whined.

Sterling ramped up through tall grass onto Main Street. He tossed a pamphlet in my lap, *How to Win Friends and Influence People* by Dale Carnegie. "Well, if you want friends, sometimes you've got to be one first." Without opening it, I looked up at Sterling like he was crazy. "It's just an idea I heard some guy pitching, but it works. It's at least worth a try. You'd be surprised what you can learn from reading. It's simple, really. We all basically want the same thing. People like when you remember their name, for instance, and something interesting about them. Then you talk about it the next time you see them." He tossed a note tablet into my lap. "I jot it all down. Go ahead, see for yourself."

He had several names written down, followed by a note for each one, beginning with the school administrators, then city officials, some of their kids, and then surprisingly, all eleven of the Newtown kids I had been playing with. Seems I was also not the only one playing dumb. My jaw dropped when I read Mike Rinaldi's name along with his brothers. I looked up my name. Next to it was scrawled: Only kid from Newtown brave enough to go to junior high in Oldtown.

"Do me a favor. Write down your weight, next to your name." Sterling handed me a pen from his vest pocket.

"What's the point?" I sat tall and stared back at this seemingly gruff man for the first time, only to be entreated by kind eyes. Then I folded my arms defiantly and buried my head in my chest. "We're never gonna play ball for you, mister." I turned away.

"Who are those kids?" Sterling pointed out a few bigger kids as they scampered out of the road and hid behind buildings.

I ducked down in my seat.

"Humph . . . Not yet friends of yours, I take it." Sterling smiled wryly.

"Those bullies? Never! That's Clay, Elmer, and X. They're fifteen or sixteen. No doubt waiting to pick fights with any kids from Newtown. You know, anyone dumb enough to try to belong in Oldtown." I stuck a thumb in my chest. "It's not a fair fight." Workers busied themselves unloading freight from the arriving train at the edge of town. Sterling weaved through the cross streets toward the school. I set the book and tablet to the side. "Can you let me out here? Pa wants me to run an errand."

Sterling thought it over. "That wasn't the deal. I get to take you to school. And from what I understand, you're not going to want to be late to Vera Mae's class, anyway." He patted my shoulder. "Tell you what. I'll buy you lunch later. We'll run your errand and maybe you can help me with an errand of my own." Sterling drove away along Vine Street toward the combined high school and junior high school building ahead.

I nodded hesitantly, looking out the passenger window, unable to look him in the eye. We were silent. He slowed the car to a stop at the entrance to the school. I got out.

"You sure you don't want to borrow my pamphlet?" He held it up.

"No thanks. I have all the friends I need." I shut the door and walked forward.

"You never asked what I need your help with." Sterling spoke up. "Just point me out a few houses, is all."

I didn't look back. I didn't need his help. And I didn't want to help him. I walked into the school building, pushed through throngs of anxious, talkative students, and then walked right out the exit doors at the other end of the hallway.

2
Town Friction

At the corner of Main Street and Vine, I focused my attention on the town square. I proceeded cautiously, relieved that I was already behind enemy lines—west of East Street, the dividing line. A couple cars passed by each other on streets wide enough to turn around a team of horses pulling a wagon, just like in Salt Lake City. Several cars were parked at different storefronts. There weren't any people on Main Street, but three Smith boys. Sam, Willis, and their cousin, Ivan, amused each other in a car right outside the music store on an adjacent street. Two of them were dressed in the accepted school attire for older kids: dark trousers, buttoned white shirts, and flat black fabric hats. The other wore more everyday attire, similar to my normal everyday wear: knickers and knee-length socks. Through the foggy glass windows of the Tooele

Mercantile Company, I saw a clock hanging on the wall; it was ten minutes before eight. I hesitated, looked at the Smiths, back at the clock, and then walked slowly.

I edged past the Utah Power and Light sign hanging over the walkway. I focused beyond my destination on the Chevrolet dealership, with all of its new shiny black-domed cars. I inched past the Tooele Rug Company, underneath the drab, brown, tent-like covering that extended from its roof. Then I hurried across the street into the music store. Mr. Tom Greene greeted me and offered any help if I needed. Mrs. Smith looked through some school supplies near the wall of records. A couple girls in modest school dresses, accented by pink and blue ribbons in their hair—one blonde and one brunette—giggled at me from an adjacent row. Mrs. Smith found that amusing. I didn't. I looked away and busied myself quickly picking through record titles. Finally I found the one I was looking for: "Always," by Irving Berlin, sung by Henry Burr. By now the two girls were at the front of the store, still giggling, scrawling something on a paper with a pen they had borrowed from Mr. Greene. As I waited in line behind old Mr. Ferguson, the blonde giddily handed me a folded note, grabbed the other giggly girl by the hand, and tugged her free of her shock and out of the store with bouncy steps. The front read, "to Gerald Gillespie," who happened to be my best friend. I wondered if they realized that wasn't my name. I bought the record and slipped out of a side entrance to the music store, undetected by the Smith kids.

Shouts sounded from the direction of East Street. Contrary to my better judgement I raced into the alley next to the Rug Company and maneuvered slowly toward the commotion on the opposite block.

Clay, Elmer, and X were in a standoff with Travis Savich and Gus Karabatsos. "These kids bothering you, Gus?" The big seventeen-year-old Yugoslavian stepped in front of the small barely eleven-year-old Greek kid. Clay pushed through the broad shoulders of his perpetual bodyguards. Clay and Travis stood nose-to-nose glaring at each other, neither so much as quivering. I was stiff with fright.

Gus and Travis were in working attire—coal-stained overalls and mining boots. Gus's overalls hung loosely on his short, scrawny frame. The olive skin of his dark, freckled face squished under a pair of glasses set on his big rounded nose, accenting his dark black curly hair. Travis looked as foreboding as any adult coal miner, with his large bony frame, stern chiseled face, and short spiky hair. Clay, Elmer, and X were husky boys wearing soiled jeans and farmer boots.

Skipper Gowans and Kenneth Shields filed into the street from behind the trouble: five boys now surrounding the two. "What's going on?" Kenneth asked.

"You know darn well what's going on. This Dago stole Skipper's bike and spread his newspapers all over East Street." Clay stared Travis down like a prosecutor goading a confession. I looked around but didn't see any newspapers strewn about.

A voice echoed behind me through the alley. "Keep up, Ivan," Sam Smith yelled.

It would soon be eight against two. I crouched out of sight behind cement stairs and wooden crates stowed at the side entrance to one of the buildings. Sam ran by first, his cousin Willis following close behind, and then Ivan finally straggled past.

I hurried back to my spying post at the corner of the Rug Company's red bricks.

"Skipper, tell them he didn't take your bike." Kenneth Shields stood tall with his wiry frame but stately presence. He was wearing a clean, nicely pressed white collared shirt and bowtie above a vest, shiny black slacks, and slicked-back hair, looking as though he were running for mayor.

"Don't ask me. I don't know who took it." Skipper spoke bitterly, restoring his suspenders to his thin shoulders and straightening his glasses under his newsboy cap.

Clay shoved Travis. "Yeah, but we know who's going to give it back."

Sam and Willis got in front of Elmer and X, keeping them out of the fray.

Kenneth stood between Travis and Clay, separating them with his forearms on their chests. "That's what I'm trying to tell you!" Kenneth yelled, facing Clay directly. "We found Skipper's bike and delivered the papers. Everything is fixed."

Elmer held his hands up. "Fixed? Newspapers don't scatter themselves."

"Do you know who did that, Skipper?" Sam asked.

Skipper shook his head. "The transcript bulletin gave me authority to deliver its paper. No one else has permission." He stared at Kenneth.

"I was just helping you. Do you know who scattered the papers to begin with?"

"No, but who else would have?" Skipper looked up at Travis and Gus.

Ivan turned and looked in my direction. I pulled my head out from view for a second. When I peeked again, Ivan was quietly talking to Skipper, who pointed questioningly toward me.

"We don't mean trouble. We just came to buy work supplies," Gus said in a squeaky, but coherent voice. Travis said nothing, just continued his cold stare of disgust.

"Not today, you aren't. We don't need your money!" Clay said, indignantly. "But we will take it if you don't get out of here," he threatened.

"You and who else?" Travis stared down the others.

"You're outnumbered." X pushed by Willis.

"What do you guys have against us anyway? We're just doing what we're told," Gus said awkwardly, ducking behind Travis.

"Yuh ain't doin' as you're told very well! We told yuh ta get outta here, didn't we?" Elmer stepped forward, with Sam holding his arm loosely.

Clay stared down at Gus viciously.

Gus looked pleadingly at Kenneth Shields to restore order. Kenneth shrugged. "Well, you two didn't choose a good day for it."

"Shouldn't you guys be in school?" Travis asked. "Look, we didn't take no bike or newspapers. Come on, Karabatsos, let's go. They can't stop us." Travis moved Clay aside with the ease of one arm. He disappeared into the General Store. Gus tried to keep close.

"There's gonna be a fight, sooner or later. Ferriners have been stirrin' up all kinds of trouble. You don't belong here," Clay yelled after them.

I leaned harder against the corner of the building that I was braced against trying to hear as the boys grumbled in hushed tones, but the old wall's bricks were loose. One pushed free and I toppled to the ground with a thud.

"Who's that?" X asked. "Not another one."

"Hey, Bohonk, you aren't welcome here!" Elmer shouted in a gruff voice.

"Go back where you came from!" Clay shouted, leading the charge as the boys started to run in my direction. I felt my beating chest with my hand and looked around warily. There was no use running. I got to my feet slowly and was surrounded by the time I dusted myself off.

"Hey, haven't I seen you at church?" Ivan asked as he caught up to the group.

No use telling them I was new to the area and asking for directions to school.

"You know this kid from church?" Willis asked.

"Well, yeah, I think I've passed the sacrament to him a few times," Ivan said.

"Yeah, I go there sometimes." I looked at Kenneth hoping for some help, not disclosing that he was my cousin. He stood back, quiet and pale. Kenneth and I had an agreement that no one in either town needed to know we were cousins.

"Did you see who took my bike and papers?" Skipper asked.

"No, I don't know anything about it. Truthfully!" I stared him straight in the eye.

"What's this?" X asked. He ripped the packaged cylinder from my hands.

"Give that back!" I swiped at it, but X handed it off to Elmer and pushed his hands up into my chest, holding me away.

"You want it?" Elmer asked. I nodded.

"Then buy it from your own town." He dropped it to the ground and stomped on it, smashing it into pieces.

I tried not to tear up, going to my knees to collect remains.

"What did you do that for?" Sam Smith asked.

"Pioneer stock built this town. We're not gonna let anyone take what belongs to us again. Let 'em have Ophir and Mercur," Elmer said.

"Don't bring the pioneers into this." Kenneth shook his head.

The school bell began to toll, ringing louder and longer, eight times in all. "Everyone for himself!" Clay exclaimed. Clay, Elmer, and X scattered. Skipper followed.

"I'm sorry, Joe. I gotta go." Kenneth gave a helpless look and then ran off.

"Maybe the store will replace it," Sam said.

"Or maybe they'll think we did it," Ivan said.

"We'll say he dropped it or something." Sam bent down to help pick up pieces.

"You would do that for me?" I was dumbfounded.

Mrs. Smith stepped out from the corner of the Mercantile Company. "I thought maybe you boys ran on to school so you wouldn't be late. Sorry it took me a little longer than—" She quit fumbling around in her purse for a moment. "Who's your friend?" No one replied.

"Would you like a ride to school?" Mrs. Smith looked inquisitively at the broken fragments of record in my hands and on the ground.

I didn't say a word. I let the pieces fall from my hands and just ran off. I cried at the train depot as I counted the spare change from my pocket. Ditching school that week was going to make for some of the longest days of my life.

☙

Saturday morning I secured the gate to the chicken lot and rushed back to the house with a basket of eggs. "My chores are done." I rested in the doorway. "Can I go play pass ball now?"

"Your Ma and I are real proud of you. A whole week of school without pass ball: go have fun." My dad kept reading from an old newspaper. "You know I ought to go work in Ophir. They found more gold over there."

"Ophir? What happened in Ophir and Mercur anyway?" I asked.

"What do you mean?" Mom untied her apron, placed it on the table, and sat down next to Dad.

"Some kids in Oldtown were saying the pioneers got overran there."

"I think you mean the extermination order from Missouri," Mom said.

"Well, they kind of did in Ophir and Mercur too." Dad looked up. "Colonel Patrick Connors was a man brought in by the US Government. He established the first claims in the 1860s. And just as Mormon communities appoint their own as leaders, Connor's didn't appoint Mormons over his towns. Ophir was named after the city of gold in the Bible, but a promise of riches attracted saloons, brothels, and plenty of people not interested in the Mormon way of life. So the Mormons mostly left it to the outsiders."

A chicken squawked as it scurried under my legs. It flapped its wings against chairs and fluttered around the table creating quite a ruckus. Dad dropped the paper in amazement. Mom screamed.

I ran after it and trapped it in the corner. Then I grabbed it by the neck.

"Did you forget to close the gate?" Dad asked. "Are there more loose?"

"It flew the coop!" Gerald Gillespie poked his head around the corner.

"Gerald! You about gave me a heart attack," Mom shrieked. She grabbed Dad's paper and chased Gerald around, swatting him.

Gerald laughed in a way only he could. "You should have seen your face."

I handed Dad the chicken. "Gerald, Ma is not going to let me around you anymore." I tackled Gerald onto the couch and rubbed my middle knuckle on his head.

"Here, come get this chicken." Dad spared Gerald more punishment.

Gerald and I went outside. "I got something for you." I gave Gerald his little note.

"What's this? Who's it from?" He read it out loud. "Come to the dance."

"A blonde girl from school handed it to me, but I don't know if she wrote it."

"You don't even know her name?" He crumpled the paper into his pocket.

I shrugged. "I'm not making too many friends." I shut the gate and tied it closed.

"Well, I'm not going to any dance," Gerald laughed, "Wanna hear something funny?" He placed his hand on the nearest post.

I looked up at his mischievous smirk. "What did you do?"

"A couple of us guys wanted to surprise the newsboy on Monday and deliver his papers. You know, just to see what he would do." He snorted, unable to contain himself.

I shook my head and looked at the ground in disbelief, smiling at Gerald's typical antics.

Gerald nudged me a few times. "Only the kid didn't think we were being very helpful. When he spotted us, he starts yelling. We had to toss the papers on the ground and get out of there, but then the wind blew them all over East Street. Funny, huh?"

"Are you kidding me? I almost got beat up for you." I grabbed Gerald by the front of his collar and shoved him. "I was trying to buy something that day."

"You too? Don't tell Travis Savich. He's out for blood!" Gerald kept laughing. "He thinks they were lying about the whole thing. A whole group of us kids are going down there on the eight o'clock train." Gerald straightened up. "You should come."

"You're going?" I stepped back. "And you're not telling them what you did?"

"You can't tell anyone. I'm serious!" Gerald became jittery.

"Can't we just buy stuff without a hassle—like normal people?" I reasoned.

"If we go as a group, there won't be a fight." Gerald reassured.

"Or it will be worse. But I need to go. It's my mom's birthday today."

"It's your mom's birthday and you haven't got her anything yet?"

"No thanks to you!"

Gerald was grinning. I gave him another shove. "Gerald, those thieves took the record right out of my hands and busted it to pieces. I used up most the money Dad gave me to buy it."

The grin left Gerald's face. "What are you going to do?"

"Now I'll have to sneak a copy, at least until I have the money to buy it, again."

"You have no way of earning money." Gerald's face mirrored my desperation. He was as serious as I had ever seen him. "What if Mr. Greene catches you stealing?"

I paused for a moment. "The way I figure it, Oldtown owes me a record." Then I barged back into the house, Gerald trailing. "May I go to Oldtown with Gerald?"

Mom was busy changing the cloth diaper of George, the cooing two-year-old. She was telling Dad about something that Jack, at just eight years old, had done in a game of jacks earlier that day: collecting five jacks in a single swipe.

"May I go to Oldtown with Gerald?" I repeated.

"Your mother and I were talking. You can politely wait your turn." Dad bounced the ball and picked up a few jacks to the delight of his clapping eight-year-old boy.

"I don't want you going to Oldtown on the weekends." Mom shook her head.

"Not even for church?" I snidely remarked. Everyone fell silent for a moment.

"We're meeting up with some kids from church that go to school with me." I knew that would appeal to my mom, and also what would appeal to my dad. "Some of them play on the football team."

"You want to play football with those kids?" Mom asked, skeptically.

"No kidding? Well, I say anytime a Newtown boy gets a shot, he should take it." Dad winked at me. Mom and Dad exchanged long hard looks.

"Gerald and I got invited to a dance," I blurted out, grabbing the paper that Gerald had retrieved from his pocket to mull over the handwriting of the four-word invite again.

"I'm not going to no dance." Gerald grabbed his paper back.

"It's not until later this evening, but someone has to set up for it," I went on.

"A dance? Now, that's more like it. All you yellow-bellied men in here should take a shot at a chance like that."

Dad started laughing. "I think she's got us there. That's one scary proposition."

Gerald looked sheepish. Mom about busted a gut.

A knock came at the front door. It was Sterling Harris, hat in one hand and a gift in the other. I invited him in. He handed me a record. "You left this at school. Just thought I would bring it by." He waved to everyone inside and nearly turned to leave.

I was in shock. I looked at Gerald who appeared as surprised and relieved as I was.

Dad got up from the floor. He came over and shook Mr. Harris's hand. "You came all the way out here just for that?"

"Oh, it was no trouble. Mrs. Smith actually brought it to me. I told her I would be in the area. We're on an errand, looking at apartments." He waved back at his wife, waiting in the car. "Peter, you ought to take your wife to the dance tonight in town."

"You're a troublemaker, mister." Dad smiled. "Actually, I'm making my wife a birthday dinner tonight. And Joe here has a surprise we got for her."

"Oh, happy birthday, ma'am." Sterling looked over at me, clearly realizing now what the record was all about. I kept it concealed behind my back. "Say, that's one of those nice radios," Sterling said, looking around my dad's shoulder. I slipped the record onto the turntable.

"The baseball game is about to start. Joe and I always listen together."

"Who's playing?" Sterling asked.

"You want to check it out?" Dad started tuning the radio.

"I better not. Maybe another time." Sterling placed his hat on his head and left.

Dad leaned up in the rocking chair and tilted one ear close to the dull, silver box.

WJZ transmits the game by telephone to a station in your area. We broadcast the team nearest you. Stay tuned for the—

Each word that came from the box sitting atop its own shelf was accompanied by static. The radio whirred as Dad tried to turn the combination-like spin dial for better reception. He pressed his ear against the cold metal top where TRF was inscribed on a gold triangular plaque with Atwater Kent 35 labeled above that. Four gold rivets framed the plaque in the center. Dad kept turning the dial and listening to the box; he looked like he was a thief trying to open a safe, but his efforts didn't improve the sound.

Welcome, Baseball Fans. The St. Louis Cardinals are about to take the field. The anthem has been played, and the visiting Philadelphia Phillies are set to bat.

"Can you hear it well enough?" Dad asked me.

"How can you even tell if they're playing a real baseball game?" I asked.

Dad laughed. "Good point! Only water shortages seem to come in clearly!"

Mom threw a cloth diaper at Dad, hitting him right in the forehead. I dodged the other one she threw. We had to explain the inside joke to Gerald—how Mom had mistaken our neighbors' intentional damming of our shared dike with their silent protest over our loud rooster as a drought, and then how she had run frantically outside to warn the very neighbors that were stopping the flow.

"You guys never said if I could go to town or not," I reminded them.

"Joe, don't you want to be around to celebrate someone's

birthday?" Dad looked at the turntable instead of the radio he had been adjusting.

"And what about our team? The Cards are playing right now," Dad continued.

"Oh, you just want him to listen to that silly squawk-box with you. Don't mind me. I won't make you miss a dance. Go help your friends prepare for it." Mom grabbed a pair of my socks from her pile of things to be sewn or mended. "You go get ready. I'll darn your socks. I was going to have them ready for Sunday, anyhow." She sat happily admiring me for a moment. "Your first dance!"

Dad sat aghast, in disbelief. "You're going to let him go all day long? What else have you and Gerald got cooking?" Dad asked. We stared back at him. "Oh, all right, you just be sure and make it to church in the morning with your mom." The whole family went with Dad to the occasional mass around Easter and Christmas, but even though he never came to church with us, he always encouraged me to accompany Mom. I went with Mom out of pity more than anything. I thanked Dad and then gave Mom a kiss on the cheek.

3
Oldtown Dance

Several of us kids exited multiple sidecars. Travis Savich led the march on East Street. The Oldtown kids were waiting, ready for us.

"I can't believe you lied to your parents." Gerald smirked.

"What do you mean? We're meeting up with Oldtown kids right now, aren't we?" I laughed. "And *someone* does have to set up for the dance." I knocked Gerald's cap off.

Three boys crouched in a semicircle on the other side of Main Street ahead. Elmer and X flanked each side of Clay as they got to their feet. Clay spied our army coming down Vine Street first. He yelled out over his shoulder: "Boys—East Street is the boundary to our town. If any ferriner crosses, pelt 'em." A host of boys came out from their hiding places behind buildings and trees. They stood over piles of rocks clawed from the earth; both their hands and longs were soiled at the knees. Clay spoke sternly. "If I were you, I'd turn right back around." Clay reared back and chucked the first rock just short of our feet.

Travis Savich picked it up and handed it to Joe Rinaldi. Joe smiled, wound up, and hucked it well over our intimidators, bouncing it down the road. Everyone froze for a moment, watching to see if a store owner would notice.

"We can take these guys," Travis roared. Boys rushed about picking up rocks and heading for cover. A flurry of rocks flew from the Oldtown side. Newtown boys returned our sparse fire in hand and then gathered rocks that had been thrown at us. Seeing us out in the open retrieving their rocks only encouraged an onslaught of more projectiles.

Elmer stepped out from behind a tree and took a rock right in the eye. He covered his face and went to the ground. It prompted an immediate ceasefire.

"Who threw that rock?" Clay demanded.

"Oh, come on! It's a rock fight! Anyone of us could have thrown it." Travis walked toward Clay. He was tossing a rock up and down in one hand.

"There's no throwing at the head!" Clay yelled as he helped Elmer to his feet.

"Oh, so now you have rules for throwing rocks?" Travis asked.

"This is our town," X said.

Ken Gillespie whispered to Gerald and me. "Come on, guys. Let's go see what's playing at the theater. They don't need us to sort this out."

"I don't have a dime on me." Gerald pulled the inner pockets out from his longs.

Ken countered, "Have some faith in your older brother."

"Good thing no one needs to buy a record." Gerald patted me

on the shoulder. "No one will be buying anything here on Main Street." Shop owners were turning the *Closed* signs out in view of the mounting mob of kids.

Ken started walking around a building and motioned for us to follow. "We'll just see what's playing is all. Then we'll come right back." Ken had recently turned sixteen years old.

"Oh, I get it," Gerald said. "You just wanna stare at Roxy Lee." We skipped up next to Ken. Gerald tried to get in front of Ken's view as he kept walking around him. "I thought you didn't like tag-alongs," Gerald taunted.

"I don't. I invited you guys. There's a difference." Ken shoved Gerald.

"Milt will never let you date her," Gerald said as got in his brother's face.

Ken smiled confidently and pushed past him. "We'll see about that!"

We weaved through rows of brick buildings, across empty, dirt intersections. All the storefront windows were layered with a film of dust, and not one car passed us on the street. The theater was larger than most other buildings in town and stood alone in its own city block. "So this is where all the adults went," I said. The only cars we had seen all day were parked in a row extending along the back-side of the theater and along the street. A line of males and females gathered to see the matinee. A sign above the entrance read "See Buck Jones and Tom Mix every Saturday." Music from the hands of Roxy Lee played on the organ just within the open entrance, adding sound to an otherwise silent moving picture. It was the finale, and her hands danced thunderously over the piano keys. Occasionally, her enthusiasm forced her to bump her brother, Milt, with an elbow to the back. Milt was sitting perpendicular to her in order to watch the movie; he looked at her disgustedly over his shoulder each time she elbowed him but didn't say anything to her.

"See!" Gerald pointed. "You can't talk to her with him there." Gerald shook his head slowly. Ken didn't react. "He's so lucky! A free movie, whenever he wants it." Gerald and I gawked at the long line and those who could afford to stand in it, while Ken pondered the situation. Suddenly Ken tucked his shirt in, strapped his suspenders back over his shoulders, and combed a hand through his hair—pushing it in place as best he could without the use of a mirror. "How do I look?" he asked us. Gerald looked around him, practically on his tiptoes looking over Ken, trying to scan the line.

"Why? Who? Roxy?" Gerald looked stymied.

Ken shook his head. "Nope."

"Then who?"

"You'll see. Quit making a scene." Ken pushed down on Gerald's shoulders with both arms. "You two stay here. I'll be back soon."

Ken walked smoothly toward the line of people. Three girls, dressed in stylish summer frocks with ribbons tied about their waist, stood in the line talking to each other, or at least appearing to be engaged in an important conversation; they acted like they didn't notice Ken until he verbally interrupted them. All three girls perked up. Two of them were the girls my age from the record store. He spoke to them confidently, orchestrating motions with his hands. And with each gesture they giggled. One girl pushed at his shoulder, flirtingly.

"What do you think he's saying?" I asked Gerald.

"I don't know," Gerald said, kicking at the dirt.

Then Ken pointed us out to the girl his age, Annis Crandall. "He's pointing at us," I told Gerald.

Gerald looked up, somewhat alarmed. The girls looked at us and waved. We waved back, shyly. One blew a kiss at Gerald.

"What do we do?" Gerald asked.

"That's the girl who gave me the note," I said.

"Don't fool around!" Gerald insisted.

"I'm not kidding!" I laughed.

Gerald punched me in the arm before standing at attention for Ken's return. I winced but smiled as I rubbed my arm.

"What was that all about?" Gerald asked, a little flustered.

"What? Those girls? They're members of that prestigious girl's club, the Rusty Dozen!" Ken looked proud of himself. "They want to see us at the town dance tonight."

"Really?" My mouth was agape.

"Roxy is in that group," Gerald said.

"Exactly!" Ken smiled, slyly.

"But I can't dance," I blurted out and stepped backward.

"You can't dance." Gerald started laughing uncontrollably.

"What's so funny about that?" Ken asked.

"All this time, you've been pushing to go to that dance, and you can't dance?" Gerald went on. "All those excuses to go to town and now you're stuck, aren't you?"

"Ah, it's easy enough. Girls show you how anyway." Ken's eyes searched my petrified expression. "I've got an idea: that shop that sells records in town. They've got a turntable phonograph. We can go practice some swing steps there. I'll show you how." He paused and held his hands out. "Well?"

Gerald looked at Ken with disbelief: "Are you kidding me?"

"No one has to know." He messed up Gerald's hair with his hand and Gerald tried to withstand his brother's longer reach to return an attack on Ken's perfectly combed hair. Ken laughed. "A few dance lessons couldn't hurt you, either."

"Shut up," Gerald said, his face turning red.

"It'll just be us three." The brothers relaxed a moment; their arms at their sides.

Ken looked at me while maintaining peripheral vision of Gerald. "Well?"

"All right, but—" I started to say, but Gerald cut me off.

"All right? All right, he says. You're as bad as him. A couple cute girls and you're all in." Gerald shook his head.

"So you think they're cute, huh?" Ken teased.

"I didn't even change clothes for this ruse!" Gerald patted dirt from his jeans.

"Are you sure it's really open to everyone in town?" I asked.

"There's only one way to find out," Ken said.

Oldtown would have to accept me eventually, on account of my mom growing up there, but I wanted strength in numbers, not just to be tolerated and alone. It was a long shot, but if the dance went okay, they might go with me to school on Monday as well.

"Well, all right, what are we waiting for? Last one to the record shop is a rotten egg." Gerald skipped ahead.

"Why are you suddenly all excited?" Ken asked.

"We found someone who's bound to dance worse than me," Gerald said.

Ken laughed. "Don't count on it."

☙

Most of the boys at the dance were in the same attire they wore to school and to play in, except none had hats so they could keep their hair slicked and parted. A few wealthier boys wore wool blazers. The girls came mostly in paisley dresses. Many had ribbon bows tied along their dresses. Several wore fancy silver or white dress sandals with heels. Other girls wore flat, black dress shoes with sewn and patched dresses. Ken led Gerald and me to the girls he had spoken with earlier at the theater. The music began to play through the large phonograph turntable record player set in front of a bulky TV style microphone on stage. "Well, we came here to dance guys." Ken turned from us. "Want to dance?" Ken asked Annis Crandall.

"Yes, I would," she said in as proper a tone as she could muster. She curtseyed and tilted her head, her lashes fluttering as she spoke.

Gerald followed suit, imitating his brother as best he could, and escorted the blonde, Millie Kurtz, to the dance floor.

I shifted my stance and looked beyond Mary Whitehouse, the brunette girl who remained, then looked straight ahead, then right at her. She giggled. I looked at her nervously a few times more and she smiled each time I did, but she never looked at me directly for very long. After a seemingly long pause I shuffled closer and managed to open my mouth, but no words came out. I'm sure I looked queasy.

"Do you dance?" she asked.

"Em, yeah, well, no . . . I mean yes. I'm not really sure." My mouth smacked with dryness. I quit talking before anymore words fumbled out.

Mary put a hand to her mouth and giggled. "Well, who doesn't know if they can dance or not? I'll teach you. Just follow me." She took up my left hand in her right hand. I reached with my other hand to place it on her back, only I was too far from her and my hand planted firmly in her armpit. Mary's eyes widened and then a smile expelled the shock on her face. She then moved in closer and guided my right hand to a position on her back just below her shoulder blade. "Now we're ready," she spoke properly as she placed her left hand on my shoulder.

Mary taught me how to dance the waltz to an elegant piano composition. I stumbled through the motions, but Mary just laughed and reassured me until the end of the song. We kept dancing, and she taught me snappy steps for brass band music. I was learning quickly how to dance and laughed at how goofy Gerald's awkward moves still looked. Gerald was still with Millie. Ken was with another girl and kept eyeing any other girl that danced past his view. Mary and I stopped abruptly as she pointed out what had become the focus of everyone else's attention; it was Sterling Harris and his wife.

"See how well they dance together? They glide as if they don't even know anyone else is around," Mary said, obviously enamored with it like the rest of the girls in the room.

Sterling's wife gaily tapped through swift steps; her movement filled with youthfulness and exuberance. Sterling led their motions, but he tried to keep up with her. The beat picked up and they leaned back away from one another keeping each other balanced by holding hands at the end of outstretched arms. They continued to perform swing steps at a quickened pace until the music stopped abruptly. Cheers and loud applause burst out from the circle of onlookers. The couple in the center of it all paused for a moment with great big smiles, their faces turning red as they caught breaths of air. Sterling's wife looked wide-eyed at the crowd that had gathered. She curtseyed to them and waved with embarrassment, putting her reddened face in her hands, in between waves. "Folks, this is my beautiful wife, Viola," Sterling said, unabashed.

The next song to play was "Always," the tune I had bought for my mother.

"Oh, you must dance with me again, Mary." I took her by the hand. "My mom loves this song. Teach me how to dance to it."

"You already know how," Mary said. "Dancing slow is easy." She moved closer to me than before, her cheek next to mine. I closed my eyes as we danced. As the song ended, I looked over her shoulder and saw Ken dancing, once again, with yet a different girl.

"Could you excuse me?" Mary nodded as I left for the water table. Clay, Elmer, and X had just motioned to Kenneth Shields to come over to them. All of them approached Milt Lee. Wayne Hanks stood conspicuously around one end of the water table eavesdropping. I positioned myself in front of the barrel of water and dipped the wooden drawing spoon deeply as I reached for a metal cup.

The boys spoke softly. Only Milt didn't care if anyone heard him.

"Who did that to you?" Milt stretched a hand toward Elmer's swollen black eye. Elmer moved away.

"Gus Shields." Elmer pointed him out.

"Let's get him back," Milt said. "Rocks will be the least of his problems."

The boys lined up behind me to get a drink, but their backs were to me.

"Shields? What gives? So he's related to Kenneth?"

"My last name's Shields too!" A lanky blonde-headed kid named Lloyd piped in. "I'm Kenneth's cousin, but we're not related to Gus."

"Man, this is confusing. I don't know enough to know who's with us and who's not. Are there more of them here?" Milt asked.

I quickly drank my water and threw my cup past Wayne Hanks, who was cowering on a chair next to the bin of dirty cups; he flinched at the flight of my cup as it fell like a rock and clanked into the bin. I shuffled back behind the boys to make an inconspicuous retreat.

"You bet, Ken Gillespie is dancing with your sister," Skipper Gowans squealed.

"We'll have to gather some bigger kids." Milt lifted his head from his cup of water. "Hey, Wayne, you in?"

Wayne shrugged but then nodded weakly.

In my haste to warn Ken, I accidentally bumped into Sterling, who was talking with Superintendent Nielsen and Principal Mills. "Oh, Joe, how are you? This is my wife, Viola."

"Pleased to meet you." Viola offered her hand and I shook it.

Mrs. Nielsen escorted Mrs. Mills over. "Viola, I want you to meet Joe Mills's wife." They exchanged pleasantries and Mrs. Nielsen tugged Viola away from the men.

"We're dying to know what you think of the town," Mrs. Mills said.

"Oh, the town is lovely. You have a theater and a music shop. I love the arts," Viola confessed. Their conversation trailed off as they got farther away.

"Have you and your wife made a decision?" Mr. Mills asked Sterling.

Sterling nodded.

"Good man! We want to announce it tonight," Mr. Mills said.

I watched, horrified, as trouble walked toward Gus Shields and Ken Gillespie.

Milt Lee tapped Ken on the shoulder. "No honkies allowed. This is an Oldtown dance." Then Milt forcefully tugged Gus by the shirttail away from his dance partner. He stumbled backward, knocked over the water barrel as he lost his balance, and fell into the grasp of Clay and X.

They held him back by both arms."An eye for an eye, right, Elmer?" Milt pushed Ken away from his dance partner, Roxy Lee. Elmer sucker punched Gus in the gut.

"Hey, hey! No fighting!" Superintendent Nielsen tried to separate the group. "Elmer, you told me it was Travis Savich who punched you in the eye."

Elmer looked down instead of speaking.

"Boys, this is a dance. Everyone's just here to have fun." The superintendent looked at each of the boys, hoping to convince them. They all looked at the floor now.

"They gotta go! They are from Newtown. That's the rule!" Milt folded his arms.

"That is the rule," Miss Vera Rae verified.

"You can't be serious?" Sterling moved a chair from his path and joined them.

"School-aged children must attend our school to come to Oldtown dances," she quoted. "Those kids will never fit in an Oldtown school system."

"Yeah, they ain't even want no learnin'. Half of 'em can't even speak no English." Clay stubbornly crossed his arms, his eyes wincing with each bitter word.

Miss Vera Rae rolled her eyes, shooting Clay a disappointed look. Gerald snorted.

"Let's go! We can't speak no foreigner here!" Ken mocked Clay as he pushed past Milt. The room was deathly silent, watching as Ken, Gus, and Gerald left.

Miss Vera Rae dismissed herself. "I'll get a towel to dry this up."

I watched for Sterling's reaction as the cultural hall returned to normal, practically unfazed. He looked amazed. Then I turned to leave also. "Joe?" Sterling said, sharply.

I quickly realized he wasn't talking to me, but rather to Principal Mills.

"That rule is bogus," Sterling said.

"This is a community event," Viola said as she and Sterling sat down with Principal Mills and his wife and Superintendent Nielsen and his wife.

"The community voted and it's only fair to accommodate those within the voting district," Mrs. Mills tried to explain. "You have to understand, Mrs. Harris. It's a delicate matter. Sure, it goes too far to make it a religious cause or something, but you can't blame folk around here for not wanting their daughters to marry out of the covenant."

Mrs. Mills and Mrs. Harris noticed me eavesdropping. That didn't stop Sterling.

"Marriage? What's that got to do with anything?" Sterling asked. "Sounds like we look after our own at the expense of state funds. We fear letting anyone else in, lest they override us!" Sterling was hot mad. "You both knew all along that Newtown boys won't be allowed to play football, either, unless they go where they aren't welcome."

"Not true! Actually, funding would go up by admitting more students, but it's just not functional. We work best as two towns."

Superintendent Nielsen kept swinging a finger and tapping a foot in time with the music as he watched the band. "It's logistical. We don't have enough room, desks, chairs, or teachers, to expand our reach for their needs. Besides, there are plenty of boys from Oldtown to field a team. I should refill the water." He stood up. "Principal Mills can make the announcement at the end of this song."

"No—no, that won't do! I won't coach unless they get a chance to play."

Mr. Mills gave Sterling his full attention. "Now look. Be reasonable. There were a lot of other candidates in town more well-known than you," Mr. Mills said. "People are comfortable with what they know," Mr. Mills continued. "You only won 50 percent of the time as coach in North Cache, by the way."

"And you know we were a depleted team because of the beet harvest. Give me twice the team, I'll give you twice the results." Sterling looked resolute.

"They must go to school first," Mr. Mills scoffed. "They won't do that!"

Sterling reached into his back pocket. "I'll make you a bet." He started flipping through bills in his wallet. "I'll get a kid from Newtown to commit to going to school Monday before the night is out." He looked once more at me—standing behind Mr. Mills.

"What are you, drunk? Mr. Harris, I hardly think that's appropriate. I'm not a betting man." Mr. Mills turned his chair slightly away to better face the stage.

"Oh, he's just kidding. He's always doing that," Viola said to Mrs. Mills.

"Lacey?" Sterling called out to me. "Joe, will you go to school in Oldtown on Monday, say, if we were to get half a dozen of your friends to go?"

I nodded. I didn't expect Principal Mills would be amused. But he let out a laugh.

"Make it a baker's dozen, counting Lacey, and you've got a deal. The loser gets to kiss one of Bevan's pigs in front of the whole school. We'll have a pep rally and properly announce your team."

Mrs. Mills and Mrs. Harris guffawed and clasped their own hands in the air victoriously with two loud successive claps. Mrs. Nielsen looked uncomfortable.

"Then it's settled. Mr. Mills, you introduce me to some of the boys at church from last year's team. Joe Lacey can introduce me to some of his neighbors who might also be interested in football. And we'll give every last one of them a proper invite." Sterling leaned back in his chair, resting his hands behind his head.

4
Newtown Recruits

Sterling started for Principal Mills's home in case he wanted to join us but changed his mind about halfway there. "Watch out!" I yelled. Sterling swerved just in time.

Wayne Hanks scurried out of our way as the dusty black car rumbled over the bumpy terrain, crushing sagebrush and pushing tumbleweeds out around the car's path.

I fell into the dashboard as Sterling stomped on the brakes. Dust curled past the automobile's big curved hood; then Sterling promptly reversed, spitting up dirt and rocks into the cloud of dust in front of my view. We skidded to a halt. Sterling promptly clasped the windowsill of the door and swung it open. He quickly pulled his robust frame up. "Wow, you move really fast for a big guy."

Wayne had nowhere to hide. "You nearly ran me over." He breathed hard, sat up, and placed his hands on his knees.

I watched as Sterling stepped in front of the car and placed his hands on his hips above his overcoat pockets, a book still tucked away in each one. A debonair hat shaded his face. "Sorry about that. I didn't expect to come across anyone out here."

Wayne looked around at the vast expanse. "You ever heard of a road?"

"You play football last year?" Sterling waved dust from the air. "With those reflexes and a little endurance, you could be quite good."

"I prefer not to get knocked around," Wayne admitted.

"Thirl, isn't it? Thirl Hanks?"

"Wuh—Wayne, sir. I prefer my middle name—it's Wayne."

"What are you doing out here, anyway, Wayne?"

"I could ask the same question," Wayne said.

"Fair enough. I'm visiting some folks in Newtown. And you?"

Wayne nervously rubbed a rock between his fingers, which he had clutched in one hand. He stopped fidgeting with the rock abruptly and covered it entirely in his fist. Then he swallowed and slowly tucked the rock into his back pocket. He stammered, "Ma needs me to buy some soup." He explained without further provocation. "We're all out, and the Newtown bakery is the only thing open on Sunday."

"Sure you're not buying it for sacrament?"

"NO! Of course not." It appeared he didn't think the wisecrack funny at all.

"Well, ain't that a kick. That's where I'm headed. You want a ride?" Sterling stepped back within the car's open door and raised one foot onto its floor. He placed a hand on the windowsill for support and cocked his head back toward Wayne. "Well, how 'bout it?" His big shoulders shrugged with each word.

Wayne hesitated for a moment. "Beats walking, I guess." He hurried around the car and opened the door, a little startled to see me sitting in the middle of the bench seat.

"I suppose you know Joe," Sterling said.

Wayne jumped into the passenger seat squarely, bruising his behind on the rock he had left in his pocket. He groaned slightly and slid forward in his seat, consciously applying more pressure to his back. I looked at him strangely. He braced himself on the buckboard in front of us. Sterling busily retrieved his keys while Wayne discreetly removed the rock and flung it out of the window. "There goes my protection."

I smirked, turning my head away from his view, and clasped at my mouth and nose to keep sound from escaping.

"You get caught running around too?" Wayne asked me. I just grinned. Wayne took that as a yes. "Yeah, I figured as much," he said.

The engine roared with a turn of the key and the car lunged forward into gear. Oldtown disappeared in the dust of our wake.

Sterling broke the silence between himself and his passengers. "I met some Oldtown boys yesterday, but no one speaks of the Newtown boys. Maybe you could introduce us."

Wayne sat bolt upright. "I—uh, don't know too many of 'em."

"What side of town should I head for?" Sterling asked.

"Uh, the bakery is up there on the right," I answered.

Sterling cranked the wheel to the right, spinning the tires and accelerating.

Wayne positioned himself in the same way as he had when he had sat on the rock, his back pressing firmly against the seat pad behind him. He looked quite relieved when they came to a halting stop at the front of the bakery. He staggered out of the car like he was collecting his land legs after a sea voyage. "Yeah, I should have walked."

The bakery's fresh aroma replaced the smog filled air coming from the smelter. The place felt like a tourist stop at the border of many different countries. Italians conversed with Greeks, Greeks with Austrians, Austrians with Japanese, Slavs, Dutch, and Danish. Sterling stepped away from his car completely unabashed. Several customers were seated in conversation just outside of the bakery. Sterling approached each one and introduced himself, Wayne, and me. Several persons inside the bakery peeked out the window between white painted letters advertising fresh hot bread and coffee for ten cents.

We entered the shop. Sterling acknowledged several persons in a row with a handshake, asking each person's name—repeating it back out loud—then stated his pleasure to meet each of them. The commotion relented and we quickly became the center of attention. Wayne couldn't help the expression that befell his face: his head to one side, his mouth partially open, and underneath furrowed brows, an obvious look of amazement at so many foreigners in one place. Sterling commented on the beauty of a few people's accents and asked each about his descent; he always followed this with a genuine and individual compliment of the person's English-speaking skills, even when some struggled. People from outside filed inside to hear what was being said; the owner of the bakery stood back from the countertop, happily counting heads.

"Twenty-three! Not bad! Not bad at all. Most we've had in here before now was fourteen. What will you have, mister?"

Sterling smiled. Then he ordered a loaf of bread. He had Wayne order the chicken noodle soup he was looking for and told us to get whatever we wanted from a row of clear plastic compartments below the countertop—filled with bread rolls of shape and fashion unlike any Wayne had seen before. Wayne marveled at the purple- and orange-colored sugar rolls. Then he ordered a couple pan de leche, calling them dinner rolls. The baker promptly tossed the rolls in a bag and handed them to Wayne without correcting him. I ordered my favorite: pan de coco. Sterling paid the fifteen cents.

Mr. Rose tugged at my shirt. "Is it true, Joe?" he said in a whisper.

"You boys from out here may actually get a chance to play on the high school team?"

"I think so, sir." I peered over my shoulder.

"Well, isn't that something?" Mr. Rose grinned. "I don't think I've ever seen anyone but smelter folk in this place," he mused, "and eating our bread, to boot." He pointed to Wayne. Wayne had forgotten himself, momentarily satisfied, as he pulled apart hot steamy bread and stuffed his hungry mouth full.

"Hmmph . . . Our bread, you say?" Mr. Savich humbugged. "The baker is a Pollock. And despite your fake name . . . you're Italian." He poked Mr. Rose in the chest.

"Hey now, my bread is not Polish. It's multinational!"

"Ah, don't get sore, Savich! However long any of us have to be here we oughta make the most of it." Mr. Gillespie placed a hand on his shoulder.

"Get your hands off me, you filthy Scotch." Mr. Savich spun around. "All you people pretend like our native lands aren't at war with each other."

"The Scottish are not at war with anyone," Mr. Gillespie corrected.

"Now what? Last time, all your problems were because of Serbic nations?" Mr. Petrovic stood up. Mr. Popovich settled him back into his seat at their table.

"Come on now. All of you know Greeks have the best blood," Mr. Karabatsos joked. He looked like a little runt pushing his way into the brutes' standoff.

This brought raucous laughter out of everyone.

"You mean to play some of our boys on your team, right?" Mr. Karabatsos asked.

"If they're good enough." Sterling laughed, confidently. "They'll play!"

The other men laughed knowingly. Many sat down again.

"Our boys can play push ball with the best of them," Mr. Savich voiced, proudly.

"It's called football," Mr. Melinkovich corrected him.

"I don't care what you call it in Croatia. Slavic boys won't let anyone push them around," Mr. Savich boasted, looking squarely at Wayne.

"I'm here to recruit them to school first," Sterling said.

"Now that'll be the hard part," Mr. Melinkovich bellowed in his baritone voice. "I'm Mike Melinkovich—George Melinkovich's father." He extended a large hand and shook Sterling's. "What you need to do is go see the priest."

"The priest? How long does confession go?" Sterling drew more laughter.

"The priest lets the boys play football in a Catholic summer league program. But they have to travel too far to play other teams. My boy, George, plays. He can shoo you all the bigger boys from 'round here," Mike Melinkovich said.

"Sure, why don't you take me to him?" Sterling asked, very directly.

"To my son?" Mr. Melinkovich asked, pressing his hand to his heart and moving his torso backward in awe. "I thought you'd never ask."

"Why not?" Sterling asked. "And to this priest."

"Uh, okay." Mr. Melinkovich looked around the room in surprise.

"Get my son Gus too—Gus Karabatsos. I want him in school. He's not big, but he'll play. He's a tough kid," Mr. Karabatsos spoke up with a high-pitched Greek accent.

"You forgot to mention he's not old enough," Mr. Popovich pointed out.

Wayne looked away briefly, made eye contact with me, and rolled his eyes.

Others piped in as well, promising their sons would contribute, each standing up as they spoke. One by one those present stood, pressing past one another, vying for the coach's attention.

The baker interrupted. "Here's more bread, for your family," he said, handing Sterling a steamy bag containing a full free loaf. "Do come by here again, won't you?"

Sterling opened the bag of bread and took in a deep breath. "Heavenly. I'm sure I'll be back here often." He returned his face from the open bag greeted by twenty-three smiles. "It was a pleasure to meet you fine gentlemen. We're off to meet your sons now, if you don't mind. Lead the way, Mike."

"Wait!" Mr. Melinkovich held up a hand. "First a toast to our new coach." He reached down next to his leg and pulled up a brown bag that had conformed to fit the shape of a small bottle, and then he poured a reddish-brown liquid into a couple cups in front of him.

"Oh, I shouldn't." Sterling waved the offer off.

"A little vino never hurt anyone." Mr. Rose grabbed one of the filled cups and handed it to Sterling. "It's customary."

"To success with our boys." Mr. Melinkovich held the glass up to speak and then drank the contents. Wayne looked flabbergasted. I tried not to be as astonished, but I'm sure it showed.

Sterling drank his in one gulp and put the empty glass on the table. The other people watched closely and cheered loudly the moment Sterling finished the drink. Sterling held the door open and beckoned for Mr. Melinkovich.

The faces on the men in the room were all aglow. Mr. Melinkovich grabbed his hat from the table at his side and placed it on his head. When he passed by Sterling, he tipped his hat in gentlemanly fashion and then exited. Wayne and I followed closely behind Mr. Melinkovich.

"Gentlemen." Sterling nodded his head and left.

Sterling hurried to his car, got in, and started the engine. "We'll have to be real friendly-like. Pile in," he said.

Wayne and I resumed our positions but squeezed enough against Sterling to provide Mr. Melinkovich a place to sit. "This is a fine automobile," Mr. Melinkovich said. "A real fine automobile." Sterling just smiled.

"Where are we goin'?" Wayne asked, hesitantly.

"You heard the man. The Catholic church, of course." Sterling smiled.

Wayne looked away uncomfortably.

"Don't worry, I'll have you back before church begins, before I pick up my wife."

☙

Sterling parked the car at the Catholic Seminary building. We stepped out of the car following Mr. Melinkovich. We stopped at the sight of dirt flung toward us from the shovel of a sturdy kid in overalls, his back to us.

"You've made good progress, Gus," Mr. Melinkovich said.

Gus Shields looked quickly over his shoulder. "Oh hey, Mr. Melinkovich. I didn't notice you guys back there. Who are you with?" Gus asked as he stepped from the trench he had created around the Seminary, his overalls covered in mud and muddy water lathered on his arms and hands.

"Gus Shields, meet Coach Sterling Harris. He'll be coaching Tooele High this year," Mr. Melinkovich said.

"Oh." Gus nodded. "Good for you!"

Sterling offered his hand to shake.

"I'd shake your hand, but—" Gus displayed his dirty palms.

Sterling reached out and grabbed it. "I'm not afraid of a little dirt. What year are you in school?"

"I'd be a freshman if I were going to school." Gus reached up as if to push hair out of his eyes, but remembering his muddy hand, he lowered his arm and blew the hair away with his mouth. He bent down and scooped another shovel of dirt.

"Shields? Isn't that Irish?"

"He should know." Gus nodded his head in gesture toward me. "Of course, some of us Shields probably don't know much about potato digging."

"I'm sorry, Gus. I tried to warn you guys at the dance," I said.

"Don't worry about it. I know my place," Gus stomped up another shovelful.

"How much do you weigh?" Sterling asked.

"About a hundred and seventy-five." Gus didn't look up from his task.

"No kidding! You and I are the same weight," Sterling told him. "You going to play football this year?"

"I play for the Wildcats." Gus wiped his brow with the back of his hand.

The Catholic priest exited the building and joined us in the beating sun.

He wore a flat hat with a circular bill, sturdy slacks, a buttoned suit vest, and shabby, pointed-toe boots all of the same dark black tone. A gold chain swung out from the bulge of a breast pocket, wherein a pocket watch was attached to one of the vest's buttons. "I saw you coming over the hill. I'm Father Kennedy. Is there something I can do for you?" He tilted his head inquisitively and stared sincerely at Sterling through perfectly round glasses.

"I brought these gentlemen to see our football team, Father," Mike bellowed.

"Sterling Harris is the name." Sterling extended a hand to shake. "This is Wayne. And you probably know Joe."

"It's nice to meet you, Wayne. And yes, Joe, we've missed you here at the parish school the past few days." I realized Father Kennedy's concern, in spite of my silence in return.

"I'm looking for some good-sized boys to fill positions on the high school team." Sterling looked over Father Kennedy's shoulder, about forty yards away, where two huddles of boys stood on either side of a football. The two teams broke from their huddles and stepped into two lines, matching up man for man opposite one another. The quarterback snapped the ball to himself.

"Whose team did you say?" the priest asked in disbelief but then didn't wait for a response. The priest looked toward the field of boys regrouping after an incomplete pass. "This team you see out here—the Wildcats—they only get to play a few games, mostly with other Catholic teams. And as you can probably guess, we have to travel great distances to play anyone. Any other Catholics play on your team?"

Sterling's attention returned. "Father, I've only been here a few days. But Tooele High School is offering me a position as the football coach. We are probably the smallest school in the district and certainly the region, but they expect me to win games, nonetheless. I figure to do that we'll need all the talent Tooele has. And that's why we're here to ask your help. It's a public school. Anyone that attends school is eligible," Sterling affirmed.

"No offense, but it's clear you haven't been here very long, Mr. . . . ?"

"Harris, Father. Sterling Harris," Sterling said. "I'd be obliged if you fill me in on some of the details though—as you see it."

Father Kennedy nodded. "Yes, well, we only have grade school out here in Newtown. Our parish are more like tutors than they are teachers. I've been trying to get those boys to make the switch to school in Oldtown, but once they reach high school age, they drop out altogether. Quite frankly, it seems that most Mormons fear international workers staying here; they group us together as, well—" He paused and looked down and then looked up again. "As Catholic impostors." His brows rose. Then he looked to the boys playing football. "Not all of these boys are Catholic; but they're all accepted here, for however long that may be—be they migrant or immigrant."

"I see. I'm sorry if it's that way," Sterling said.

Sterling and the priest both watched side by side as one of the boys caught a pass and bolted for the end zone. He shifted his hips, shedding tacklers and making others miss completely. He scored a touchdown and trotted back to his team casually.

"Wow, who's that?" Sterling asked, pointing to the scorer.

"That's my boy, of course," Mike Melinkovich said proudly.

The priest grinned. "You shouldn't boast. But he does always get picked first."

"And the shorter kid on his team, without a uniform, I would guess he's Gus Karabatsos." Sterling pointed and then looked at the priest confidently.

"Why yes, how did you know that?"

"I spoke with his father at the bakery. That's where I met Mike." The priest considered what Sterling was saying for a moment.

"You know, Father," Sterling went on, "not too long ago, I attended a school for football coaches taught by Knute Rockne of Notre Dame. Now there are a lot of Catholics, but I reckon you've heard of him. Catholics play football right well from where I'm standing." Sterling motioned with his head in the direction of the Wildcat football team, his hands securely in his pockets, elbows out. "May I talk to them?"

Father Kennedy looked impressed. "I don't see why not. It will be some kind of trick getting those boys to go to high school, but ultimately, it's up to them to decide."

Sterling took off walking in the direction of the boys. We all followed.

The boys stopped and stared at the people approaching them. Wayne watched where he walked instead of looking into the faces of the onlookers. I joined up with two boys I knew, Joe Jette and Mike Rose. "Hey guys," I said.

"Where have you been, traitor?" Joe Jette asked.

"Yeah, who are these guys? Your real friends?" Mike asked.

They turned their backs to me as I approached. "Come on, guys. You know how my parents are." Then Wayne appeared betrayed, seemingly unaware I was one of them, but I didn't explain.

"Wildcats, meet the new football coach at Tooele High," Father Kennedy began. The boys gathered closer. Sterling tugged at the priest's sleeve and whispered in his ear.

"Correction. He's not the football coach yet, but once his wife okays it, he will be," Father Kennedy added.

Some Newtown boys laughed, but most didn't know whether to laugh or not.

Mike Melinkovich stepped up. "Sterling learned to coach from the best."

"Yes, this is Sterling Harris," the priest boomed. "He's here to recruit players."

"That was a good run, George," Sterling asserted.

George's eyes widened as he pointed at himself for verification.

"You could be scoring touchdowns just like that for Tooele High School, against the best in the state. Your dads brag about all of you playing football, but I'll have to see you in school first." Turning his attention toward Gus Karabatsos, he continued, "I met your dad too."

"So you'll let me play?" Gus asked the coach before Sterling could continue.

"Well, let's not get ahead of ourselves. I expect all of you to try out for the team. I need experienced players like you guys. Father Kennedy says you play for a summer league. Come to school tomorrow; practice is after school." Sterling looked at the different faces as they looked uncertainly at one another. "What's the problem?"

"The last thing we want to do is play with those Oldtown boys," Joe Rose spoke up, arms folded across his chest.

"We ain't welcome there," Travis Savich said.

"Everyone is welcome on my team." Sterling walked up to Travis. "But I don't coach players that are too afraid."

"Who said I'm afraid?" Travis said, vehemently.

"Easy, Travis," Father Kennedy urged.

"Then I'll see you in class tomorrow. What's your name?" Sterling asked.

"Joe Rose, sir."

"I'll tell you what, Joe: if anyone tries to get in your way, I won't let him step onto my football field."

Joe looked directly at Sterling's steady eyes and nodded.

"We new guys need to stick together." Sterling walked up to the other players individually and asked each their name, how much they weighed, and what position they generally played. He jotted it all down on a pad of paper. There were Melinkoviches, Mitchells, Del Papas, Saviches, and Sullivans among others.

"If Gus Karabatsos is the only one who shows up tomorrow, I'll be sorely disappointed in some of you bigger kids," Sterling said. That drew a laugh.

"Hey, I can hold my own," Gus defended.

Danny Savich laughed and shoved Gus into Tony Del Papas.

"Yeah, believe it or not, the little runt can play." Del Papas pushed him into Gus Shields's protection.

"Practice starts tomorrow. I know some of you are too young, but everyone here is invited, if only to watch at least. I'll collect roll from the teachers every day. Be on that roll or you can't play."

Several of the kids didn't look convinced. "Shouldn't we vote on it or something?" Ken Gillespie asked.

"Sure, yeah, go ahead," Sterling said. Father Kennedy nodded his approval.

All but Wayne Hanks and the adults huddled up. A few in the middle knelt on the ground as if drawing up a play in the dirt. We discussed it in hushed, albeit agitated tones. Then Ken reported the results. "We only took votes from the older kids. It was close, but definitive—seven to six—the majority is opposed! We love football, but it's not worth it."

Sterling nodded. "Aw, just one more? Well, I have to respect your decision."

Mr. Melinkovich appeared just as dejected. I know I looked glum. Even Wayne seemed put out and kicked at the dirt.

"How many of you would change your mind if I told you there won't be a summer football league next year? We're too short on funds," Father Kennedy spoke out.

One by one all the hands went up.

Sterling fell to his knees and threw his hands to the sky, and then he jumped up and hugged Father Kennedy right off his feet. "Father, you really let me sweat it out there for a moment," Sterling said, still looking into the sky.

5
Setting a Saintly Standard

Sterling held the door open to the Tooele First Ward of The Church of Jesus Christ of Latter-day Saints. He ushered us in: Viola, my mom, and me. Skipper Gowans, who was decked out in a nice suit and bowtie, handed each of us a program. I looked at the talks that would be given: Brother Wayne Hanks, Word of Wisdom; Brother Loren C. Dunn, Love thy Neighbor as Thyself; Bishop Rowberry, Love the Lord thy God.

Roxy Lee played prelude music. Sister Rowberry practiced directing music and gently sung the words. She was immersed in it.

Should you feel inclined to censure / Faults you may in others view, / Ask your own heart, ere you venture, / If you have not failings, too. / Let not friendly vows be broken; / Rather strive a friend to gain. / Many words in anger spoken / Find their passage home again.

Do not, then, in idle pleasure / Trifle with a brother's fame; / Guard it as a valued treasure, / Sacred as your own good name. / Do not form opinions blindly; / Hastiness to trouble tends; / Those of whom we thought unkindly / Oft become our warmest friends. ("Should You Feel Inclined to Censure," *Hymns*, no. 235)

We were early, so there were only a few families seated, but the bishopric and the speakers were set to go. Sterling was pleased to see how many young men, in white buttoned-up shirts and ties, were already there fulfilling their responsibilities: preparing to administer the sacrament. He told Viola to go ahead and find us seats and then went to speak with the boys. Viola was clearly pleased to see Mrs. Mills and they exchanged friendly waves. We settled down just a few pews back from the deacons. "I'm going to speak with Mrs. Mills for a moment," Viola said and patted my mom on the knee as she dismissed herself.

Sterling shook the hand of each boy: teachers arranging the sacrament table, priests seated behind the table, and deacons in front of it. He told them how proud he was that they were there so early fulfilling their duties. Then Sterling went over to talk with Principal Mills. The congregation steadily filled the chapel.

A white-gloved hand tapped me on my left shoulder. "I thought you were twelve. Aren't you old enough to pass the sacrament yet?" It was Mary Whitehouse.

"I haven't been baptized a member of the Church," I admitted.

"Oh, I'm sorry. I didn't know that." She leaned back, removing her hand.

I smiled at my mom and she smiled back kindly. "Who is this lovely girl, Joe?"

I introduced Mary and she confidently came around the pew, sitting down next to my mother and talking with her like they were longtime friends. She admired my mom's shawl and asked her if she could show her how to make one herself someday.

When Clay, Elmer, and X finished setting the sacrament table, they did not go to sit with their families but rather sat behind the deacons just a couple pews in front of us. Their conversation caught my attention.

"I thought he was going to scold us," I heard X whisper.

"I just don't think we need them," Clay whispered back.

Elmer agreed. "Yeah, we would have enough for two teams if they play."

"Brother Harris is a hypocrite. Wayne saw him drink wine in Newtown," Clay said.

"Where do they get it? Drinking's illegal," X asked.

"Well, the local bootlegger, of course, Harry Karapolis," Elmer said, "It all comes through him, ever since the prohibition started."

X nodded. "None of us had fights till those Newtowners came either."

Clay looked confused. "No, we still fought."

X chuckled loudly. "Oh yeah, I forgot."

Clay shushed him. "You wanna get us in trouble?"

"He's not the only Mormon to drink a little," Elmer said.

"He's not the only Mormon to swear, either, but who cares?" Clay argued, forgetting his volume. Clay looked up to find Brother Dunn standing over them and staring right at him.

He shushed them. "Please, remember to be reverent in the house of the Lord." He walked back to his seat on the stands.

"I think he was talking to you," Elmer snickered to Clay.

"Shut up. He was talking to all of us," Clay retorted in harsh whisper. "Quit fooling around before he catches us again."

They sat tall now, no longer whispering. Clay looked to one side. He wiped sweat from the newly formed creases across his pale forehead. It was the first time I had seen Clay intimidated.

As all of the congregation suddenly quieted, Mary Whitehouse cordially dismissed herself back to her seat. She gave me a flirtatious wave of the fingers. Bishop Rowberry stood up at the pulpit and the program proceeded as outlined.

ଔ

The Newtown boys changed in the toilet room; they left their school clothes on the floor. The Oldtown boys took advantage of the adjoining locker room to change. All wore scrubby clothing—each resembling farmers or hobos. No one even owned spiked shoes.

One by one, each boy stepped from the locker room onto a tall, big-faced scale.

"Lloyd Shields—140 pounds, right?" Sterling said. The scale then registered at 140 pounds.

"How did you know that?"

"I remembered. You told me when I met you." Sterling did this with every boy, checking the scale to be sure and marking it in his notes.

"Joe Rinaldi—145."

"Coach, I don't want to go by Rinaldi."

"Isn't it your name?" Sterling asked.

"Could you refer to me from now on as Rose? It sounds more American."

"Sure. It's your name; I'll call you by whatever you want, just like X over there. Actually, I respect that. Everyone listen up! You are in America and the official language here is English. At our practices I expect you to know and speak English. Now I realize many of your families may or may not plan on staying here long, and a different language is spoken in your home. But if you want to be treated like an American, at least speak the language. All right, let's take this outside."

Once everyone had gathered outside, Sterling's countenance

changed from a cordial expression to one of business. "Line up!" he yelled. The boys formed a line in front of Sterling. At one end were boys from the Oldtown and at the other end were the Newtown boys.

"I was glad to hear all of you made it to school today. Some of you had to put up with me in class already. Either way, we are going to be seeing a lot of each other, so get used to it. I don't care where you're from. It doesn't matter who your parents are. You don't play unless you follow my rules." Sterling stopped for a moment. Some of the boys had relaxed their stance, looking at the ground or swinging their arms in boredom. "If you haven't paid attention to anything I've said—hear me now. If you want to play, I will have your full attention." The entire line of boys straightened their postures and looked straight at Sterling as though he were an drill sergeant. "Rule number one: In order to practice you must attend school. And if you don't practice, you don't play. Oh, and anyone that keeps another person from attending school will not practice. Rule number two: Come to me if there are any problems at school. All of you will do well in school. If you get in trouble for breaking school codes, then you are in trouble with me. Rule number three: Never be late. Rule number four: There will be no fighting—absolutely no fighting. Rule number five: No one is to drink or to smoke. Rule number six: Your family, your team, and your community come before yourself, and in that order. That brings up rule number seven: I'm aware that not all of you are allowed to go to Oldtown dances; therefore, none of you will be able to go. Your curfew is now ten o'clock, anyway." Coach rambled through all of the rules pausing only for short breaths.

There was a slight moan from Gerald's brother, Ken, after the final rule, and Gerald looked and smirked at me from our comfortable position lying on our bellies along the sideline. I smiled and he rolled over on his back and started laughing. I tried to cover his mouth, but he resisted me. Sterling moved in front of Ken. "Is that understood?" Ken looked at the football still clasped in the coach's hand and then nodded his approval.

"If you want to be good football players, you are going to have to learn to sacrifice. I will make sure you follow the rules. Your teachers and your parents work for me now.

"We will learn by repetition. If we don't get something right, we will do it again. Wayne Hanks—what was rule number one?"

"Uh," Wayne stammered with his mouth hanging open, his wide-open eyes glazing over.

"Fast. Everything we do must be fast."

"Attend school, Coach," Wayne said.

"Good. No excuses. Everyone, what is rule number two?" Sterling scanned the faces of his team. He had their full attention. "Anyone?"

"Come to you, Coach, with school problems," George Melinkovich answered.

"Good job, George. You just came through for your team. What rule is that—putting others first?"

"The rule about our team before ourselves," Kenneth Shields said.

"Which is?" Coach Harris lumbered in his direction along the row of boys, now holding the football behind him as he went.

"Rule number six, Coach," Kenneth said without flinching.

"I'm impressed," Coach Harris said, facing the team. "But I don't want one person to do the work of an entire team. When we play football, only one of you will have the ball at a time, but each of you better be a part of every play. Let's review. Rule one: attend school; rule two: come to me with problems in school; rule three: never be late; rule four: no fighting; rule five: no drinking or smoking; rule six: your family, your team, and your community come before yourself; and rule seven: no dances. Now repeat it together. Rule number one?" Coach Harris had the team repeat the rules in unison until he was satisfied that they remembered them all.

"All right, boys, let's move on. I am going to expect everything you've got. And then I'm going to expect a little more. By the end of this year, all of you will be men. We are going to have tough practices and you will have to come prepared. You will play by my rules and every play will be your best." Sterling reached for a whistle hanging around his neck. "Line up on that sideline." Sterling pointed to the line in front of Gerald and me. "I want six of you at a time. We are going to run sprints to see how fast you are."

Sterling jotted notes down after each heat. He matched different rotations of kids together and compared them. He then paired groups of six on six for line work and took notes. Sterling acted as the quarterback and called the play dead when he saw enough.

"Set, hike!" He yelled. Bodies collided and crunched, again and again.

Tired bodies slammed against one another. The whole line stumbled into a pile after one of the plays. "Get off me, Wop," Clay yelled, shoving Tony Del Papas.

Sterling pulled Tony free by his britches. "Yeah, wop," Sterling laughed. "That must be short for 'wallop'? Again. Different boys." No one readily volunteered. "Let's go!" Sterling said.

Several boys got in their stances against one another—six from one town and six from the other.

"I'm going to bust you good next," Joe Rose leaned over and told Clay.

"Oh, another Wop," Clay said, snobbishly.

Joe lunged at Clay, before the play, knocking him to the ground. Elmer and X rushed to Clay's aid, pushing other boys away.

Gus Shields reached in and pulled Joe loose. "He's not worth it."

Elmer and X stepped away, fearing Gus.

"All right, that's good for today." Kids collapsed onto the bench and lay on the ground. "I'll see you all tomorrow for a real practice, except you two, who are staying. I meant it when I said, 'no fighting!'" Sterling pointed at Clay and Joe Rose still trying to square off with each other. "You two, wait here for me. We'll conduct sprints when I return. You can still run after dark, after all." They sat at opposite ends of a bench.

Everyone else started to leave. "What about you two?" Sterling pointed to me and Gerald standing comfortably off to the side. We were the only younger boys curious enough to come watch the high school practice. "You guys want to be my assistants?"

"Don't you mean ball boys?" Gerald asked.

Sterling paused. "Yeah, something like that."

"I'm not sure I want to be part of the football team," I whispered to Gerald.

"We'll try it out," Gerald said.

"Follow me," Sterling motioned. He led us into the high school to a cabinet in his classroom. Inside he pulled a tin can with white paint and a brush. He handed the can to Gerald and the brush to me. "This idea just came to me. We are going to paint this football white, so we can see it in the dark; that way, even when the sun goes down, we will still practice."

I shot a quick look at Gerald. He started laughing.

"What's the matter?" Sterling asked me. "What's so funny?" He looked at Gerald.

"None of those guys will last through a practice that long," I told him.

Sterling turned toward us, "Catch," he yelled as he tossed a football to me. "First we will get their endurance up. But we need to make up for no spring training. In the future, we will hold a summer camp in the mountains." His thoughts were way ahead of us. He handed two more paint cans to Gerald. Then he grabbed a bag of brushes.

We started down the hall until Sterling stopped abruptly in front of us. We could hear a meeting of people in one of the rooms. The door was wide open to the hall, with a sign that said *Welcome to the public*. "I won't allow my kid to go to school with those dang honkies," said one voice, "and play football on our team? Never!"

"I just want to know who gave Principal Mills authority to admit so many students?" a man who identified himself as the superintendent asked. "I didn't have a say in that."

"Well, that's why I came to your meeting today," Principal Mills's voice joined in. "I have no power to withhold any boy's card from state recommendation, as long as they live within the official town boundaries, which does include Newtown. But surely you members of the school board can change all that and deem them ineligible, if you want."

"On account of what?" asked one member of the board. "First, we would have to draw up a new high school boundary. And then the City of Tooele would be required to set up and fund a whole 'nother high school on their behalf."

"Says who?" the first voice asked. "Why don't we make them officially become a separate city?" I peered in enough to see Mr. Mitchell standing to speak from the public section.

Sterling burst through the doorway. "Evening, gentlemen. I hope I'm not interrupting anything important."

"Coach Harris," Principal Mills said. "No, no, you're not interrupting. How's the football team looking?"

"It's great, Joe. We just finished our first practice. The team looks like nothing you've ever seen. Oh, by the way, Principal Mills, you mentioned you had cards to submit to state for each of the players—did you get a chance to approve them with the school board?"

"Well, uh, as a matter of fact, we were just about to discuss the matter."

"Oh good. I would not want to have to go to the directors of the

State Board of Education myself, just to make sure it's understood we don't exclude people here in Tooele." Sterling stared Mr. Mitchell down. Mr. Mitchell promptly sat.

"Mr. Harris, let's be calm," the president of the school board addressed him. "Integration is an experiment that largely depends on immigrants measuring up. Three of your boys could not pass their entrance exams, basic arithmetic, science, or reading and writing." He rummaged through results that lay before him on the boardroom table.

"When do they have until to pass those exams?" Sterling asked.

"Passing the eighth grade level requirements is bare minimum even to attend high school," the president responded sternly.

"Well, they won't go back to middle school in Newtown. These boys will end up in the mines if we don't bring them up to speed."

The board members conversed quietly amongst one another for a while, then the president spoke again. "There isn't any reason why they won't be cleared to play in a game as soon as they meet the minimum standard."

"Good day, gentlemen. You'll have to excuse me; I have a team to attend to."

"One more thing, Coach," the president added. "We have argued today that your program should at least get a year or two of consideration before we re-evaluate its merits, but we will be watching, and we will hold you to a successful standard."

Sterling nodded and we exited.

6
Winning Weighs

One week later, on a Tuesday evening, players stepped onto the practice field again. No one was late. Sterling stood with his whistle in one hand and a football in the other. Today, however, he was dressed in football attire. He had a long-sleeved gray shirt with dark tan tights laced up and tied securely at his waist, holding hip pads in place. And dark brown leather cleats laced midway up his calf. He threw the football to Kenneth Shields. "I've watched you boys now for a week and Kenneth is your captain. Lead the team through the opening drills and then meet me at the middle of the field."

"Coach," Kenneth said. He got Sterling's attention and then whispered something to him.

Sterling spun around and eyed George Evanovich's feet. He did a wrestling two-legged takedown and upended George. "We've all seen those shoes. Those are not your shoes." He pulled the shoes off of Evanovich and gave them back to Rands Wiley. "Anything else?" He paused. "Now then, let's get on with practice."

Kenneth started with jumping jacks, counting them off.

"George Melinkovich, Dan Savich, and Joe Rose. Please come over here. We need to talk." Their faces dropped with the news. Coach was particularly good at English and math. He offered his own help when available but also told them he had talked with a few of their teammates to serve as tutors: Kenneth Shields, Sam Smith, and Paul Sullivan. He expected they would each continue to practice just as hard preparing themselves for their time to play and help their teammates get ready for current football games, until they could qualify scholastically.

Sterling walked to the sidelines and grabbed a long wooden paddle to wield in his hand. He let the whistle swing loosely around his neck and grabbed the roster. He walked to the center of the field and waited patiently as the team executed stretches, sprints, and strength exercises. Then the already sweaty bunch gathered around the coach at midfield.

"What is that for?" Sam Smith asked, gesturing to the paddle.

"You'll see soon enough," Sterling said.

Elmer sniggered. Clay landed the knuckles of his fist into Elmer's arm at his side. Elmer looked at him suspiciously, but one look from Clay affirmed that he shouldn't think it was funny.

"Six on six, let's go!" Sterling looked at the paper roster in his left hand and selected some names. "Mitchell, Travis 'Boney' Savich, Elmer, Kenneth, Sullivan, and Sam Smith on defense. Del Pappa, Melinkovich, Clay, Rose, X, and Ken Gillespie on offense."

The boys walked to their respective group as their names were called.

"Huddles are for dummies," Sterling shouted, "but huddle anyway for now. Get organized. Choose who will play what."

Gerald, Wayne, and I had been lying on our bellies propping our heads up at the chin with our hands and our elbows pressing into the dirt. We got to our knees in anticipation on the sideline.

Sterling discussed a play with the offense before the huddle broke. The boys lined up. Ken Gillespie was set as quarterback behind X. Sterling appeared to be focused on defense as he stood directly behind them facing the offense. The ball was hiked and Elmer was the last defender up out of his four-point stance. Before he took a step, Sterling whacked him on the butt with his paddle; he was nearly the first across the line as a result and plunged into X. X stood him up, though, and Clay managed to keep Boney from breaking through long enough for a short pass to Rose just over the top of the ensuing rush. Mitchell tackled Rose after a gain of five yards. Mud and grass covered Rose's chest.

Sterling clapped his hands in approval. "Elmer, why don't you trade spots with Boney, and line up versus Clay. Boney, I want you in a three-point stance over center like a sprinter and the rest of the line to remain in a standing position, crouching, hands up, like you were about to start a race, but more of a marathon."

Sterling gave the offense another play. X hiked the ball and Boney pushed through him, but before he reached Ken, the ball was handed off to George Melinkovich, who shifted his hips, eluding Boney's grasp. Elmer didn't get paddled either; he instead pushed around Clay's block to get into the backfield, leaving a small gap.

Sterling laughed when George went through the gap untouched into the end zone. "Good rush, but you both over-pursued. You chased George right past the secondary before they could react. We need to contain, at least slow him up—do it again!"

The offense attempted the same play and the defense held, but it took a third person to help tackle George. "We are going to practice fundamentals, starting with tackling. I am going to put you through conditioning. And then, and only then, will we return to working on plays without a huddle. We've got one week and you will be ready."

Throughout the week more players were introduced to the paddle in line drills. A stuffed tackling dummy hanging from a tree was punished relentlessly, by not only the players, but by Sterling's 175-pound frame, showing them correct form. Standing at 5'11", he was a larger man than most for the time. He schooled the players as a whole, but focused on each individually, motivating each person a little differently.

"Elmer, now you're quick off the line, but keep your head up and your shoulders square or you'll end up on your stomach," he would say during a line drill. "Sam Smith, quit dragging your knees and bust through the line.

"Gillespie, tuck your right hand in your armpit if you have to, after the hand off. The other team has to believe you still have the pigskin." He barked when George Melinkovich, the halfback, ran into a host of tacklers. "And Melinkovich, good run, but cover the ball, dang it! The entire defense is tackling you. Good work, defense! Gus, open the hole with a shoulder block on Boney. Indian blocks are for pass plays.

"We are not going to just learn our positions, but everyone else's too. There will be no confusion about who is going where," Sterling said to his tired team. "We'll start again tomorrow." The haggard players breathed heavily and slowly trudged back to the locker room.

Each day, players got dressed in unsoiled, dry jerseys and weighed in. Most dropped weight. "Eat roughage," Sterling would say as a boy stepped off the scale, "you know, raw cabbage, spinach, turnips, and such." Kenneth then led opening drills in the daylight. Sterling drilled the players, repeating play after play. "Education! Know your assignments; it's as important as anything." After a good play, he congratulated players individually and rewarded them with a nickname; it became an honor to get a Sterling nickname. And the team left the field well after dark, drenched in sweat-stained jerseys.

☙

Game day arrived and Coach Harris's inaugural season of 1926 was underway. Several Newtown kids showed up late with the excuse that they were helping clear a rockslide at the mine. An anxious crowd of both Oldtown and Newtown folk sat segregated in the stands, restlessly waiting for the kickoff. Their clothes, unable to escape the dirt and soot of their trades, easily distinguished farmers and miners. But only the complexion of a person's skin—dark or light features—distinguished the Newtown farmers from the Oldtown farmers, since the trade was common between both factions. The disparity in the stands made it appear like the split crowd was cheering for different teams, yet most of the fans were there to cheer for the home team—Tooele. Gerald and I sat with the team, which must have disappointed my dad. He sat alone with the Newtown crowd. Mom hadn't come to see the game. But the stands had many vacant spots, especially on the Newtown side with the mining problem.

"Gather around." The team formed a circle around the coach. "No exceptions. Those who were late owe me, but family does come first. Who will lead us in a prayer?"

George Melinkovich readily raised his hand, while everybody else looked away, waiting for volunteers other than themselves.

"George? Okay, George, give the prayer. And give thanks for no injured miners."

George grabbed a hand of a player at each side and each in turn grabbed the hand of a player next to them, until everyone was united. A few of the players looked at each other hesitantly, before joining hands. They leaned in and bowed their heads together.

The prayer was inaudible to us outside the circle.

"Thank you, George. Boys, you have sixty minutes to play, and the rest of your lives to think about it. I want you to play every down as if it is your last. There are plenty of good players on this roster." Sterling tapped his notes. "I won't hesitate to replace you if you aren't doing your best. Let's go have fun and win one for Tooele."

An official blew a whistle at midfield. "Coach Harris, I need your captains."

"Kenneth Shields." Sterling looked at him. "We want to receive the ball second half. Let's see what they've got first."

Kenneth walked out to the middle of the field and shook hands with the captains of Bingham High School. Coach Harris paced in front of his bench. He listed off his starting offensive and defensive players from a clipboard, mostly Oldtown prodigies.

The stands were close behind the team bench. "We only have one captain?" Mrs. Mitchell asked her husband.

"At least none of those smelter kids are the captain," he leaned over and said.

Kenneth Shields's dad was sitting behind the Mitchells, next to the Smith family. "Actually, I didn't hear him list any of the Newtown kids as a starter," he pointed out.

"Doesn't Ken play in practice?" Gerald's dad had been sitting up in a far off corner of the Newtown section with my dad but had sneaked down to the team bench.

"Everyone does," Gerald whispered.

"Why isn't he in the game?" Gerald's dad tapped him on the shoulder.

"He's the quarterback, Dad," Gerald responded. "He's on offense."

Gerald's father nodded. He wiped sweat from his brow with a thin work towel. Then he put the hand towel back in his pocket and hurried back to his seat.

"That's it, you. Get back where you belong," Mr. Searle jeered.

"Coach," Kenneth yelled as he strode back to the sideline. "We won the toss." The teams entered the field and lined up for the kick.

"See!" Principal Joe Mills began. "Smarts and experience will win out."

I looked behind me, a few benches up, to see a satisfied Mr. and Mrs. Whitehouse seated next to Principal Mills on one side and an equally approving Ms. Vera Rae Sanders on the other. Mr. Searle shook his head, unconvinced. Mary Whitehouse was between her father and mother. She smiled at me and waved prissily. I shyly waved back.

Mary Whitehouse's mom pulled her daughter's arm down. "Keep your dignity!"

I quickly turned around and faced the field. Bingham returned the ball against the wind to the twenty-yard line. They ran the ball on every play, and managed to obtain first downs until they crossed midfield. Coach Harris inserted the first Newtown boy on defense, Tony Del Papas, in at safety and a few plays later they had to punt the ball away. He added a few other eligible Newtown players here and there to tighten up weak spots and rest worn-out players as needed.

Boney Savich and Gus Shields were champing at the bit on the bench. Mr. Savich was yelling the whole first half for one of his boys to play. Ken Gillespie also sat anxiously waiting his turn through Tooele's offensive possessions, which only amassed a few yards, but nothing significant. The first half ended. Skipper scrawled a 0-0 tie onto the scoring chalkboard. Gerald and I carried water in a wooden barrel to the players. The coach of the Bingham team strode across the field at halftime to chat a little. "So I see they didn't give you much to work with in your first year, here, hey, Sterl?"

"Nah, you know me much better than that. I wouldn't leave North Cache unless I found a team I could win with." Sterling smiled. "You just wait till the second half. You'll decide that they're the best team you ever saw."

The Bingham coach put a hand on the back of his head, confused. "Whatever you say." He peered up into the disgruntled faces of the Tooele fans seated in the stands. "I hope you can convince them of that."

Sterling smiled. "I'm going to let you in on a little secret." He patted his buddy on the shoulder. "My best players came late today. They'll play in the second half."

Sterling gathered us all in and let us in on an even better secret. "Best news of the day: Ms. Vera Rae's favored student assistant, Millie Kurtz, discovered a clerical mistake. A couple transposed numbers. Turns out George Melinkovich scored a 96 percent in English assessment, not a 69 percent. He will be starting the second half."

Our cheers could have awoken the dead.

The whistle blew, signaling the second half. "George, get out there and return me a touchdown." Sterling patted George on the butt as he about-faced and ran to the back-most position to receive the kick.

A low wobbly kick flew into George's arms at the fifteen-yard line. He strategically followed blockers up the middle of the field, letting the path develop, and then he burst to the forty-yard line where Bony Savich opened a hole on the left side of a barricade of players from both teams. George streaked the remaining sixty yards for the first touchdown of the game.

Loud cheers raised from the Newtown fans. The Oldtown fans nonchalantly clapped.

Lloyd Shields stepped off a couple yards, called for the snap, placed it, and crow-hopped forward, booting the extra point.

"Good kick, Lloyd," Mr. Smith cheered loudly. Mr. Shields clapped.

"Defense—you're up," Sterling said, without showing any surprise or emotion to the touchdown. He didn't even look up at the chalk scribble of seven to zero being recorded on the small scoreboard at one end of the field by Skipper's hand.

The defense held for three consecutive plays—not budging. Bingham punted into the arms of George Melinkovich, who wove a path once again from one end of the field to the other—touchdown.

The Bingham coach called for a timeout. "Hey Sterl," he yelled. He ran partway across the field toward Sterling, while his players were still returning to the sideline.

"For heaven's sake, Sterl, take that poor boy out." He pointed over at George trotting off back to our sideline. "Can't you see he's tired?"

Sterling laughed and sent a new defense in. "Make every play your best. Don't let the first team get comfortable."

He patted the shoulders of players exiting the field and nodded his approval. Sterling patted George on the back. "You're slippery as a mink. You sure can run."

Without George in to return the ball, Bingham's kicker still kicked their next punt out of bounds just to be safe. Bingham's coach clapped in approval.

"Offense—you're up," Sterling said. A stern focused look entered his eyes. His lips became straight. He grabbed Ken Gillespie's arm. "Throw a couple."

"Uh, we haven't thrown much in practice. And Joe Rose is my go-to in pass ball."

"Look, I know you can throw well. Trust your teammates. Our system doesn't need much. Just get it there."

Ken looked out at the field hesitantly.

"Look at me," Sterling said. Ken looked up. "You're my play-caller and you orchestrate this offense, but we are going to need your arm in the future too. Read the defense. Watch how they're cheating in on the run."

"But they can't stop George, Coach."

"Today they can't." Sterling placed both hands on Ken's shoulders. "Listen to me. We develop the pass and no one will ever stop our run."

Ken Gillespie got into his quarterback position behind his offensive line. He handed the ball off to George Melinkovich. George ran up the middle. One Bingham tackler jumped on his back and another wrapped around his leg at the scrimmage line, but George stumbled free of them both, leaving them piled on top of one another. He crashed his shoulder into the opposing safety, which slowed him down momentarily, and the remaining Bingham backfield collapsed on him tackling him after a seven-yard gain.

"That's the way to do it, George," Mike Melinkovich bellowed harmoniously.

Bingham regrouped in a defensive huddle. Ken smiled at Coach Harris. He brought the team to the line without a huddle. Bingham didn't notice. Either Ken's play call at the line of scrimmage or Bingham's coach frantically waving and yelling from the sideline sent Bingham's defense scrambling to get into position, but it was too late. Ken received the hike and threw a wobbly pass to a wide-open Mike Rose. Joe Rose's younger brother stumbled to a stop, then ran back for the short pass and scooped it up off his shoestrings. Mike started running and gained thirteen yards before the safety tackled him. Tooele quickly got back to the line and Ken called out the play. He took the snap and faked a handoff to Mike running in motion from his wide receiver position. Two Bingham linemen broke through the line and charged Ken with outstretched arms. George released, letting them pass by, and Ken flung a quick short pass between them to George, just beyond the line of scrimmage. He leapt up and snagged it from the air with one hand. He then darted sixty-yards for the touchdown. Ken wiped his forehead, clearly relieved. Lloyd kicked the extra point again.

The Newtown fans erupted in cheers—jumping up and down

and shouting. Oldtown fans clapped reservedly, still not sure whether to cheer or not.

Tooele's defense stacked the middle, stopping the rush, and held Bingham scoreless. The game ended and Skipper scribbled the final score: 24–0 in favor of Tooele.

☙

Week after week, I stood outside the barbershop awaiting the new article posted for the week. More people gathered each time as Tooele became front-page news. A collection of newspapers tracked the season's results, and the best articles remained on the street boards, attached to easels, throughout the year. Only two were defeats. The final paper touted, "Tooele, 1926 division champs." "Tooele does it again: 1927 division champs," replaced its position on the boards the following year. Gerald and I felt like honorary members of the team with how we gave our utmost assistance every game. But really we were just passing time waiting for our opportunity to actually take the field.

We were passing by the barbershop one cold afternoon in 1928. The newest article's headline was "Tooele blanks Grantsville 33–0."

"Another division title in the making," I said.

"Hey, what's that?" Gerald tugged on my arm and pointed at the barbershop door. A letter was hanging there dated November 2, 1928. Gerald read it out loud.

Dear Coach Sterling Harris,

Congratulations on your latest victory over Grantsville. Your team has consistently beaten members of your division over the past few years. Our committee has reviewed your request to compete in the Utah Class A state football championship tournament and has voted in favor of your request to play as a representative of Class B football, as long as the opposing team is agreeable. Your first opponent, North Summit High School, has accepted the invitation to compete with Tooele High School in the quarterfinals. We look forward to your first appearance in our tournament.

"Do you realize what this means?" I asked Gerald.

"We're eligible to be outright State Champs this year," Gerald said.

"Gee, State Champs," I thought out loud. "Does anyone else know?"

Gerald's eyes got big and he was off and running down the street. "Wahoo!"

But the celebration was short-lived. Tooele went on to win quarterfinal and semifinal matches. Wasatch Academy received the latest drubbing, officially designating Tooele the Class B State Champs. But then the Class A representative, Box Elder, refused to play in a Final match. If Principal Mills hadn't been on board before, he was now.

My dad sat at the kitchen table that morning, gleefully reading Principal Mills's scathing remarks, as reported by the *Tooele Transcript Bulletin*:

The football season is over. The Brigham City school refuses to meet us for the championship of the state. The principal and coach prefer to let well enough alone. We are not blaming them for having cold feet under the shade of a "Boxelder," but there seems to be a habit developed up there to sidestep. We think requirements, hereafter, should be such that Division A Champs should be compelled to play Division B Champs, provided B challenges and has a record to justify its contention. We claim the honors of the state and expect the Athletic Association behind us in this matter.

Respectfully yours, Joseph Mills.

"That Coach Harris of yours is sure stirring up trouble, isn't he?" my dad guffawed, slapping his knee and setting the paper down.

When the state didn't take much notice of the shared

championship, our town didn't make much of it. The state thought we were too small to really be worth our salt flats. It didn't stop Sterling from dreaming big.

7
Player Down

Sterling also loved teaching. He figured you could only go as far as your highest thoughts. He relished the scholastic accomplishment as much as anything when Dan Savich became eligible halfway into the 1926 season. Joe Rose had to sit out the whole of 1927, but even he admitted he was smarter for it. Sterling held early morning tutoring sessions with students in need every day before school, even if it wasn't for his class subject. I showed up early one fall morning in 1928 for help with some history homework about religious tenets and holy wars. We discussed how everyone on the team seemed to be doing very well in school now.

"How's your family?" Sterling asked.

"Good, but the gas station's still not doing well. Dad's looking to sell the radio."

"How's Peg Leg?" Sterling asked. "Is he still cursing basketball for that?"

"Jack? If not for his bum leg, he would be a surefire gridder."

"What class do you have first today?" he asked.

"English History, from Miss Vera Rae," I said with a wince and a distasteful tone.

"What's wrong with English History?" Sterling asked.

"Oh, nothing, it's just Miss Rae—"

"That reminds me. Can you help the Ronkovich family with some chores this morning before school starts?" He looked at the clock. "It's not easy running a home as a single parent, you know."

"Mr. Harris." Miss Vera Rae poked her nose into the classroom. "Oh, hello, Peter Joseph, good to see someone come to school early, unlike others. Mr. Harris, one of your boys is always late. And I am going to fail him. If this keeps up, in all likelihood, he'll get suspended—or expelled."

"Miss Vera Rae, you must be referring to John Ronkovich. I was just talking to Joe about how we might help that family."

"Yes," she said, "it seems John thinks his time is more important than our time."

"Miss Rae, did you know that John's mother has taken ill? If it weren't for him, none of those five kids would make it to school. John takes care of his mother every morning; that's his situation—don't bug him anymore." Sterling shook his head.

Miss Vera Rae's jaw dropped. "Honestly, how hard can it be to get a few kids to school on time?" she huffed. She glared over her glasses but got no response from Sterling. Then she about-faced, stuck her nose up in the air, and marched away.

I raced through the town alleys and streets, waved as I passed the Whitehouse family and their team of mules on the edge of town, and headed toward the Ronkovich farm in Erda. I arrived to find John chasing a couple pigs away from the trough and back into the pen. I milked the cow and filled water barrels; I carried those to the house. John gathered some eggs from the henhouse. Then we gathered the other children. John and I each gave the youngest kids piggyback rides; the other two ran alongside us.

The only sign of people in the hallway were the posters of Kenneth Shields for Class President when we arrived at school. I peeked in the classroom. Miss Vera Rae stood at the front of the room and led the Pledge of Allegiance. John and I waited outside the door.

"I pledge allegiance to the flag of the United States of America, and to the Republic for which it stands. One nation, indivisible, with liberty and justice for all." Everyone spoke so earnestly, but I wondered if anyone else was considering the irony of the many inequities that still remained in our country. Oldtown kids had assigned seats. Several Newtown kids of mixed complexions stood along the back wall with no place to sit.

When I was ready, I opened the door. It creaked open and the stiff woman in the gray buttoned-front dress, hair tightly nested, moved from the front of the classroom to confront me; she stood with hands on her hips, a ruler extending from one hand; Ms. Rae tapped the floor with one foot. "You're late? No excuse is acceptable, but what is yours?"

"I was helping John with some chores."

"Let me see your hands."

We showed her our soiled hands. She looked us over from head to toe.

"You sure you weren't throwing dirt clods or fighting, perhaps?"

Both of us shook our heads. "No, honest," I told her.

"Go clean up. I'll reserve punishment upon your return."

We overheard Clay talking with Milt Lee. "All you've got to do is call him a honkie, or something. That'll get that hothead swinging." They were exiting the restroom and got quiet as we passed, but we had no idea who they were talking about.

"Sorry for getting you in trouble." John spoke to my mirror image.

I shrugged. "It's not your fault. Let's hurry and get back." I turned the water off.

We interrupted Miss Vera Rae mid-sentence. She stood with arms folded, started tapping her foot again on the ground impatiently, and waited for us to take our standing positions along the wall. We did so as quietly as we could, but she did not continue until we were settled.

"Everyone take out a pencil and paper. You will now be tested on what Mr. Ronkovich and Mr. Lacey have missed—the current poetry of Eliza R. Snow. Both of you will also be writing fifty lines apiece on the board after school, on how you will not be late under any circumstances, especially for fighting."

Per her request John and I returned to write lines after school. I had just completed my first ten and started erasing to do it all over again. She sat with her glasses in one hand and rubbed her eyes with her other hand. We heard a commotion in the hall.

"You're just a dumb honkie!" yelled Milt Lee.

"Don't call me that!" Joe Rose yelled back.

"I'll call you whatever I want. You're too dumb to pass a test on your own, ain't you? I bet your coach cheats for you."

Miss Rae stepped into the hallway just as Joe landed a fist against Milt's jaw. Milt shoved Joe, and then Joe tackled him to the ground.

"Fight! Mr. Mills. There's a fight." Miss Rae ran toward the principal's office.

Sterling came around the corner. Joe Rose got a few more punches in.

"Whoa, whoa, boys. Rose, what is this about?" Sterling pulled Joe free.

"He called me a honkie," Joe said.

"So what? I call you a honkie all the time in practice."

"Yeah, but you don't mean nothin' by it," Joe countered.

Miss Rae and Principal Mills arrived. "Who was fighting out here, Sterl?" Principal Mills asked.

"It was Mr. Rinaldi and Mr. Lee," Miss Rae answered.

"It's Rose. I go by Rose," Joe Rose said.

Principal Mill folded his arms. "Well, Sterling, you know what this means?"

"Suspension?" Miss Rae asked.

"Our soon-to-be-named All-American will watch another half from the sidelines."

"What about Milt?" Sterling asked.

Principal Mills scratched his head. "I reckon his dad won't be too pleased."

"That's all?" Sterling scoffed.

Miss Vera Rae looked equally put out. "Suspend them both from school."

"Now, now, we don't want kids missing school," Principal Mills said. "The school board dictates that this situation calls for corporal punishment. And any other actions are at the discretion of coaches and parents. Come with me, you two."

I returned to my position at the chalkboard. John Ronkovich never left.

☙

Dark storm clouds rolled in. Rain pitter-pattered against the window. By the time I got outside, the players were sloshing through mud puddles in a downpour as they collided at the line of scrimmage. Players knew that they had to practice to play, but nevertheless the team was shorthanded today. Gus Karabatsos lined up to rush center. Ken Gillespie was in a shotgun formation. Wayne Hanks hike flew high and slipped right through Ken's hands. Gus Karabatsos got through the line quickly, but Ken shoved him wide of the ball. Wayne Hanks recovered. Gus gave a clap of his hands realizing how close he was to stealing back possession.

A flash of light and a simultaneous boom sent all the players sprawling to the ground. George Melinkovich and George Gillespie laughed and teased each other, pointing out how scared the other was. But Gus didn't get up from the ground. He lay on his side, not moving. Sterling ran to him first. "Gus," he called out. He eased him over onto his back and listened. "He's not breathing. Joe Rose, run and get the doctor."

Everyone was gathered in. "Can't you give him a priesthood blessing?" I asked.

"Rose, I said get the doctor," Sterling repeated. Finally, Joe Rose bolted across the field, Mike Rose following. Sterling gathered Karabatsos in his arms. He pushed through the onlookers. "George, will you say a prayer with the team?" Sterling momentarily walked backward addressing us, then sprinted to the school building carrying Gus, pleading with him to hang on.

I waited outside a room sitting silently with Sterling and Viola. I watched the clock ticking. We stood up to acknowledge Mr. and Mrs. Karabatsos when they arrived. No one exchanged any words. Sterling showed them to the door to see their son.

Sterling swore and stood up. "I don't feel worthy even to bless my own family." He slammed a wall. "I'll go check on them." He went into the room.

"Don't mind him," Viola patted my knee.

"I don't understand," I told her.

She turned and considered that for a moment. "Well, Sterl appears strong to you and everyone on the outside, like everything in his life is fine and dandy, but there are a lot of hard things in life that can break a man up on the inside."

I looked at her as if to ask another question, but then I looked down instead.

"Sometimes the only way some are able to cope is turning to vices," she said.

"You mean like my dad?" I asked from my slumped position. "He smokes like a chimney."

Viola hesitantly nodded. "But people can change." She smiled, and then we sat in silence again.

This time I broke the silence. "Can I ask you another question?"

"Sure. I don't see why not," Viola affirmed.

"What does it mean to be married in the covenant?" I asked.

"Are you asking me that because of what Mrs. Mills always says?" she asked.

I nodded. "Yes! I don't understand."

"Well, okay, you want the biblical answer or the short version?"

I smiled.

"In the scriptures, you might study priesthood, covenants, ordinances, authority, but what it really comes down to is family. God's plan is for us, His children, to return to Him again." She looked at my expression and could tell my confusion at this answer. "Let me explain it differently—have you ever been to a wedding?"

I shook my head.

"Most marriages, the person performing the wedding states that it is 'until death do you part,' because that's the legal authority the minister of the wedding has. It may sound like a fairy tale, but marriage, performed in God's way, is an ordinance that can last forever. Death is not the end."

Sterling poked his head out of the room. "He's doing much better. Come see!"

Viola let out a sigh of relief and we joined the others in the room with Gus.

Principal Mills poked his head in the room. "How is he doing?"

"He's going to be okay," the doctor beamed. Gus gave a thumbs-up.

Principal Mills smiled. "You sure did give us a scare." He held his heart. "Sterling, the school board is about to discuss the football team."

Sterling put his arm on Viola's shoulder directing her from the room. I followed. The discussion in the meeting hall already looked heated.

"Gus isn't even in high school yet. What's he doing practicing boys before they are of age? I never let my boy practice in this weather." Elmer Searle's father stood complaining.

"Good, Mr. Harris is here. Mr. Harris, as you know, it is our standard practice to review how teachers and coaches are doing. In reviewing your record, a number of concerns have come to our attention with regard to the football team." The president of the board leaned on the boardroom desk, hands clasped.

"But we have improved our record every year." Sterling looked puzzled. "This year we all but took the 1928 state championship." Sterling stood front and center before the board. Mr. Searle took his seat. Viola sat in a chair near the front. I sat with some of the boys on the team scattered throughout the room.

"What we mean is there appears to be a lack of respect in the program," the president explained.

"I don't follow," Sterling said.

"It has come to our attention that some of the Oldtown boys want to quit the team," the president informed him.

"I do run a tough program, but I treat everyone the same," Sterling asserted. "I'd be happy to discuss it with any boy who thinks he can't cut it."

"Mr. Harris, we are trying to get to the bottom of this as well," a member of the board said. "This is an open meeting. We are all invested in the success of this team."

"We assume you have read the article in the *Deseret News*?" asked the president. "That's a reputable source that reaches readers across the state. It calls into question 'conduct' and 'good sportsmanship' of players and their 'irreverent,' 'unruly' coach."

"The instance in question is unfounded, but if it is in the news, it must be true."

"We also understand one of your boys was in a skirmish on school grounds today. We're not sure sitting out half a game is sufficient punishment," the president leveled.

"He took swats from the school just like the other boy." Sterling folded his arms.

"He nearly got a boy killed today." Mr. Searle jumped up and pointed at Sterling. "What about that?" Mr. Sullivan tugged on his arm.

"Don't forget he bets, swears, and drinks," Mr. Hanks shouted.

"Mr. Searle and Mr. Hanks, please, we will address every issue in turn," the vice president spoke up. "Mr. Harris, these boys are your responsibility. Per your request, we are going to grant you an assistant coach, but we will get to choose who that will be. You may use ball boys to assist your team, but they will not be allowed to practice with the team under any circumstances." He paused briefly. "Your assistant will evaluate the need to conduct practices into the night and maybe we can better avoid dangerous conditions like today."

"I am very sorry about what happened today," Mr. Harris said.

"This is a sobering reminder for all of us," replied the president.

"Mr. Harris, these boys look to you for leadership and good judgment."

"I understand," Sterling Harris said.

"I'm not sure you do understand," the president said. "What we are telling you is that if things don't improve, then we will be forced to place you on probation."

There was a low rumble of voices through the people in attendance.

"Let me get this straight. If I play certain boys more, and I work them all less, you will be more satisfied with those results. This is a winning program! Best in the state!"

"You can't fire your winningest coach!" Mr. Melinkovich bellowed.

Another rumble circulated.

"Please, please settle down. No one said anything about playing certain boys or firing anyone." The president stood up. "Of course we want you to win games, Mr. Harris, but it also matters how you win games. What keeps me awake at night is wondering if those we hire are the best influences for these boys."

Sterling faced the crowd. "I'm just a football coach trying to win games, but I promise we will commit to appropriately representing the school. That said, who among you will be with us when we win an outright state championship?"

After a pause, Kenneth Shields stood up. "I'm with you, Coach." One by one the football players followed their captain and came to Sterling's side. Last, Clay, Elmer, and X reluctantly joined. Sterling faced the school board again, as if challenging them.

☙

Sterling invited my dad and me on a horse ride one lazy Saturday morning. We got a kick out of the recant by Les Goates, editor of the *Deseret News*, for "a gross error in judgement in airing opinions, unwarranted by subsequent facts disclosed, about your football team and its coach." We had scarcely returned when Kenneth Shields pounded on the front door of the house. "Coach Harris, come quick!" Kenneth yelled when he saw us with the horses in the corral. Kenneth Shields and Ken Gillespie ran over to where we were.

"You two are here early this morning." He scanned their faces. "Slow down. What's the matter?"

"It's Mike Rinaldi," Ken Gillespie finally said.

"Doctor says he's in bad shape." Kenneth Shields stepped away from the house beckoning with his arm. "He might need a blessing. We need to hurry."

My heart sunk within me. And my throat knotted. Sterling mounted his horse once more.

We rode the horses along planted rows of cottonwoods, through empty streets, and walked into the doctor's home. Sterling slowly opened a door to a room. He stepped in. The doctor gently covered the boy's face with a sheet. I watched Mr. Rinaldi fall to his knees and bawl into his hands. Tears streamed down my face. The doctor shook his grieved face at Sterling. "What happened?" Sterling asked.

"His appendix burst." The doctor lowered his head. "I was too late."

Sterling moved to Mr. Rinaldi, picked him up from the floor, and comforted him with an arm around his shoulder.

☙

Sterling kept an arm around Mr. Rinaldi during the viewing for his child. And Mr. Rinaldi held his wife close on the other side. They stepped away from the casket. The entire integrated team lined the back wall of the viewing, dressed in church attire. Newtown members walked in and give their respects and then sat quietly in the pews of the Catholic Church.

Joe Rose walked up alone and stood before the open casket. "I'll miss you, brother. We'll always remember you."

Sterling walked up and put a hand on Joe's shoulder. Joe turned into him, and they hugged. "We were supposed to finish the season together."

"I know," Sterling said.

"I'm dedicating this coming season to him." Joe released from the embrace. "My name is Joe Rinaldi, Mike Rinaldi's brother, and I am going to finish my football career as a Rinaldi—so all the papers know it. So everyone knows it!"

Sterling embraced his crying player. "I'm sure Mike will know it too. And you know what else? You're going to lead us as team captain this year."

My parents arrived, and I joined them and sat with them next to Viola, where Sterling had left her. Sterling sat down next to his wife after accompanying Mr. and Mrs. Rinaldi to a pew at the front.

Sterling whispered to Viola, "I can take you home now, if you're in pain."

"I want to stay," she whispered back.

Sterling looked around. "There isn't one adult from Oldtown here."

Viola whispered to him again, "We don't know their circumstances. Maybe they're just too uncomfortable to be here."

"That's no excuse," Sterling whispered back. "Things have to change." Sterling hunched forward in disappointment.

"Well, your players are here. That says something. Parents may not have formed those bonds yet, but they know their kids have. They know you've served and loved their kids. It makes a bigger difference then you'll ever know."

Father Kennedy addressed the Newtown audience. "Thank you all for coming here today. It is good to see so many friends supporting the Rinaldi family."

Bishop Rowberry and his wife entered. He nodded at Father Kennedy and quietly sat down in the back. Mr. and Mrs. Mills soon entered and sat down next to Sterling.

"Thanks for coming, Joe. I am sure glad to see you here." Sterling shook his hand.

Principal Mills sat up straight and listened intently to Father Kennedy.

8

Eating Grass

The 1929 state finals arrived. No team had so much as scored a point against Tooele all year. There was no way anyone was going to deny our team at least a shot at the Class A title.

I got off the dark-brown bus—labeled in red letters as East High School, but filled with the Tooele players. Sterling led the way. I followed the team. The players stared in awe at the large field and stands. The opposing team jeered them as they walked past the boys stretching out. "Not exactly a cow pasture, is it?" one of the boys said. "Or a coal mine," said a second boy.

Clay countered, "It isn't that great!"

"Oh—tough guy." The first changed the inflection of his voice to stress the words.

"No, he just didn't understand you—talk slower," said the second. They laughed.

Clay fumed, his face turning red. But no one else seemed to care about the other team. Elmer walked next to Clay to shield him from the opposition.

"Does your bodyguard play for you?" the second boy said.

Boney Savich stepped up to the boy. "They don't work in the coal mine—I do; you have a problem with it?"

No response.

"I didn't think so," Boney said. He walked away and caught up with Clay.

"See, it's not so bad having me on your side for once," Boney told Clay.

Clay looked relieved. "Its better than putting up with them."

"I'll take that as a compliment." Boney and Clay smiled.

The players found their bench and surveyed the University of Utah stadium seating and all of the fans. Their mouths hung agape in awe. The place was packed.

"How's Viola, Coach?" George Melinkovich asked.

"She's tired of being pregnant." Coach lifted a foot up onto the bench next to his two-year-old son, Richard, and bent down to tie a shoelace that had come undone. "She'll be okay with your mom looking after her." Mike Melinkovich sat alone in the stands. "Tonight is no time for a letdown, fellas. This is it. Leave no doubt! We all know we have a tough opponent, East High, over there," he pointed to the other sideline. "They have no respect for us. They don't think we deserve to be here. I doubt they want to play us at all. But they don't have a choice. The whole state wants them to win, to put us in our place. No one has scored on us all year. Don't let them be the first."

I walked over to the coach and helped unload equipment. Sterling handed me a football. "Here's our game ball." I went and handed it to the head referee.

East hurried down the field after the kick and tackled Joe Jette at the thirty-yard line. Ken Gillespie handed the ball off to Guy Mitchell, the fullback. He picked up two yards. A pass to Joe Rinaldi was knocked down on the following play by one of the opponents guarding him. On third down, Joe Jette was handed the ball and went for four yards. Joe Rinaldi punted. The kick went straight up and landed untouched twenty-five yards away; it rolled in favor of Tooele for five yards and stopped on East's thirty-five yard line.

East came out throwing on the first three downs, completing passes to three different players. They gained twenty-five yards and two first downs. On their first run, the halfback broke through the middle and picked up fifteen more yards, getting tackled at Tooele's twenty-five yard line. Sterling switched out the entire line. Mr. Gowans, the newly assigned assistant who was dressed in his best vest and business suit, was feverishly taking notes of the substitutions. "I don't want to panic. Is it always this exciting?" he asked. X took Clay's position next to Del Papas instead of Boney Savich, and Wayne Hanks returned to center in place of Gus Shields. On the other side of Wayne stood Elmer and Paul Sullivan. Del Papas made the first tackle for a loss in the game, pulling the quarterback down on a keeper.

"Get used to it," Del Papas warned, sprawled on top of the quarterback.

East's quarterback shoved two closed fists into Del Papas's chest. "Get off me."

Del Papas promptly got up and lowered a hand to lift the quarterback to his feet. The quarterback refused him. Del Papas held his hands up like he had been innocent of a bank robbery, only he smiled smugly. "That's all right; I'll be back."

The ball was hiked from the thirty and East's halfback took the handoff running away from Del Papas's position. Paul Sullivan came off the end and threw him down at the line of scrimmage. His dad celebrated in the stands. East lined up in the single back formation, allowing the fullback to line up for a pass. The quarterback received the hike and bodies clashed at the line. He dropped back and threw the pass, but Del Papas swatted it down at the line. East passed up the forty-seven yard field goal attempt and lined up in their T formation. With fourth down and fifteen yards to go, they passed the ball again, but Del Papas knocked it down at the line.

Tooele took over on its thirty-yard line. Joe Jette rushed for three yards, then four yards, and three again. With first down from the forty, Ken Gillespie kept the ball and dove through a different hole than Jette had taken, fooling most of the East players, for another five yards. Jette ran through the line untouched on the following play and Ken tossed him the ball; he was taken down after seven yards and another first down. Ken lined everyone up again and called the play. He tucked the ball and ducked his head down, but he was stopped at the line of scrimmage on the opposing forty-eight yard line. He handed the ball off to Jette, again, but East's entire line helped force him to the ground at the forty-seven yard line. Third and nine more yards to go. Ken looked to throw the ball to Joe Rinaldi, but two men were keeping with him, so he turned and threw to Ivan Smith, hitting him squarely in the back. Tooele punted. Sterling nervously paced the sideline as the defense barely held up, and the offense struggled, never getting into opposing territory for the rest of the half. He kept returning to the water jug in between possessions and drinking water. And he picked grass and chewed on it nervously.

The first half ended at 0–0. Sterling gathered the men together. "None of you are breathing hard enough. All of you are going to play in this game. I need you to give it all you've got on every play, and then come out, rest for a play, and get back in. Don't save anything!" Sterling nervously rolled a piece of grass in his fingers, staining his fingertips green. Sterling spoke to Ivan Smith. "I guess you didn't expect that last pass."

Ivan grinned and shook his head. Ken laughed and grabbed Smith by the shoulder. "Sorry about that! We'll get it back."

"It was a good idea, though. They are covering our main targets," Sterling said.

"They are holding us," Joe Rinaldi said.

"No excuses," Sterling said. The team took the field again, and Sterling stuck the end of a piece of grass in his mouth and uneasily chewed on its stem.

The third quarter was hard fought. Both teams played as hard as they could. Sterling crouched over the grass and rotated people in and out after every play. With each rotation, another piece of grass went into his mouth. By the end of the third quarter, his tongue was stained green and his teeth were specked with bits of green grass. In front of him, a small patch of dirt was exposed where grass once had been. The only time he left his crouched position was for his frequent visits to get more water.

The fourth quarter began and the bare spot in front of Sterling became wider and wider. He was focused on the game and continued rotating players with each play. With eight minutes to play, Ken faked a pass to Joe Jette out of the backfield and threw the ball over the middle to Ivan Smith; this time he caught it on the run and carried it to the opposing twenty-yard line. On the next play, Ken handed off to Jette, and Jette burst through the middle, then avoided secondary tacklers by shifting his hips and jumping to the side of outstretched hands; East's safety received a hip to the forehead and fell flat on the ground. Jette sprinted right down the middle of the field and split past two defenders as they collided with one another and fell down. Sterling threw his handful of grass upward and cheered, and then Jette, looking up at Sterling's excitement, ran head on into the field goal with a thud. His momentum carried him over the end line for the score. Everyone quit cheering for a second, and Joe Rinaldi ran into the end zone. "Jette, you okay?" Joe Jette sat up and held the football out victoriously. Cheers erupted. The extra point was good. Tooele was up 7–0.

"Jette, you looked like George Melinkovich out there, right up until you rammed into that goalpost." Sterling put a hand on a bump protruding from Joe's forehead. "Are you sure you're okay?" he asked.

"Scoring a touchdown made me forget the pain."

East went three plays and punted.

A few exchanges later, Tooele was winning the field position, but had to punt; the ball bounced out of bounds at the four-yard line. East's quarterback came from the sideline with a few players; he joined the rest of his offense, who were slowly returning from blocking on special teams. The quarterback formed a huddle in the end zone and many of his players used the moment to catch their breath. They stood, hands on hips, and stared blankly—no one person looking in the same direction as another, and no one focused on their quarterback. Sterling's men waited, ready at the line. The quarterback hiked the ball. X ran through the line and chased East's quarterback out from the pocket. He set himself to pass, brought the football up behind his ear, looked at X, who was getting closer, and tucked the ball and started running. Del Papas slammed him down at the three-yard line. He extended his hand to help the quarterback up, and the quarterback looked away, denying him. Del Papas shrugged. "Remember me?" he said as he walked off the field for Clay to come in.

East didn't replace anyone. Boney Savich broke through the line when the ball was hiked. The quarterback bent over for the hit and Boney planted a shoulder into his side, creating a bone-crushing sound and popping the ball loose into the air; the quarterback landed a few yards deep in the end zone, and Del Papas snatched the ball out of the air for another touchdown. The kick was good. 14–0 was chalked onto the scoreboard. With a few minutes to go,

East High had a good kick return, a nice reverse play, and broke loose on a pass play, barely stepping out of bounds when pushed by Pennovich at the 8-yard line. Their quarterback handed the next few plays off quickly, bulldozing down to the one yard line, but taking up valuable time. They lined up again. East was all but defeated. Tooele was on the verge of history. There was only one point of suspense that remained. The announcer pointed out how the last play of the game could ruin Tooele's string of shutouts. East looked determined. They hiked it from the I-formation and handed it off to the fullback, running behind their running back, but they were met with a bevy of Tooele players for a crushing loss and a final blow. Time expired. Tooele High was officially the 1929 state champ. We cheered so loud that, if it were possible, people back in Tooele would hear us.

Coach Harris went to shake hands with East High's coach, but he didn't oblige.

"Thanks for the game, Coach. You gave us a scare," Coach Harris said.

"You were lucky. That's all." East's coach walked away, grudgingly.

❧

The bus let us off at Tooele High School. Sterling was giving me a ride home but he wanted to check in on Principal Mills first. "Looks like Mr. Mills could use our help." Sterling parked and then walked toward the Mills's property gate.

Mr. Mills was sitting on a hay bale with his head in his hands. His milking cow was lying on its side at his feet.

"Looks like your cow came down sick, Principal Mills? Mind if I take a look at her?"

"Well, I'm out of ideas! I can't even get her to move into the barn for the night. She won't budge." The cow moaned as Mr. Mills pulled on its neck.

"Do you have any buttermilk?" Sterling asked.

"Well, sure, but what for?"

"If we can get the cow to drink it, it will cure its belly ache. We'll have her up and walking in no time. She probably just ate some bad grass, is all," Sterling said.

"I can't lose my milking cow. The school doesn't pay that well." Principal Mills paced back and forth.

"Don't worry yourself, Joe," Sterling said calmly. "Everything will be fine."

Principal Mills went and got the buttermilk. Sterling administered the medicine and the cow slowly lapped it up. He rubbed the cow's belly.

"Maybe you should drink some!" I told Coach Harris.

"What does he mean?"

"Coach eats grass when he gets nervous," I laughed.

"Oh, the game! I can't believe I haven't asked you. Did you win?"

"Of course we won, Joe! No need to be nervous!" Sterling beamed.

"We shut 'em out!" I said, as though I had anything to do with it.

"Well, it doesn't get any better than that, does it?" Principal Mills. "Wooooohoo!"

His yell echoed in the valley. "That's the greatest news since striking gold in these parts!"

"I just hope the town recognizes what the boys have done to put us on the map," Sterling said.

"Oh, how could they not? The expectation of it has been all the rage around here for days!" Principal Mills exclaimed. "Are you sure this will work?" Mr. Mills eventually asked.

"Just give it some time." Sterling kept rubbing the cow's stomach.

None of us knew what to say more. We just enjoyed the peace of the evening.

Finally the cow expelled a loud burp, filling the air with an awful stench.

"Gross." Sterling's son, Richard, stepped back. He'd practically gone unnoticed until then.

"She's going to make it. She'll be a little weak tonight, but now we need to get her up and keep her walking for a while." Sterling stood and pushed on the cow upward, while Principal Mills tried to lift the cow from the front torso. The cow stood up slowly.

"That's amazing!" Principal Mills stroked the cow's side.

Wendall Mills came walking up the lane. "Hey, you guys missed the parade!"

"There's a parade?" Sterling looked at an equally oblivious Principal Mills.

"Yeah, there was. Well, kind of. Most of the Oldtown folk have been celebrating on East Street," he said. "It was kind of an impromptu thing, I guess. The school band came out. Town folk were hoisting the football players on their shoulders."

"Well, why didn't anyone think to tell us?" Principal Mills asked.

"I guess we figured you knew," Wendall said. "Everyone just told their neighbor or at least the people they home teach."

"And the Newtown players?" Sterling asked. "Suppose anyone told them?"

Wendall looked dumbfounded. He shook his head. "I don't think so. At least, I don't recall any of them being there, anyway. Everyone got caught up in the excitement, is all. I mean, it wasn't like we planned it that way." He looked sheepish. "Gee, I'm real sorry!"

"Well, doesn't that beat all." Sterling started laughing. "Guess my home teacher doesn't know who I am," Sterling joked.

Principal Mills shook his head and laughed. "Mine, neither! What can you do?"

"Anyway, Wendall, I hear you are just back from your mission. How was Minnesota?" Sterling asked.

"Not bad. It's just cold enough that people sometimes forget themselves and let Mormons in. I would say the spirit of prejudice is giving way to a spirit of indifference."

Sterling nodded. "Well, I need to get home." Sterling shook their hands. "Will you be okay taking it from here, Brother Mills?"

"Yes, indeed. You should get home to your wife. Thank you so much for your service." Mr. Mills started walking his cow toward the barn.

"You know, I knew something must be wrong when we didn't see you at the game. That's why we stopped by," Sterling said.

"Sorry I missed it. I know it had to have been extraordinary. Your games always are," Principal Mills said.

"Wish you could have seen it. I won't forget those boys' faces. It was a great send-off with all the boys graduating this year."

"Sterling, can I ask you something? What happens when you start losing?" Principal Mill looked grave.

"What do you mean?"

"Well, you will have a lot of young boys this coming year. They could never justify firing a winning coach, but a losing one?" Principal Mills told him.

"Joe, level with me. What exactly does this town want from me?" Sterling asked.

"Would you like me to wait in the car?" I asked uncomfortably.

"Ah, they don't know what they want." He paused. "To tell you the truth, I didn't always like you, Sterl. You can be brash and arrogant." He stopped again as Sterling's head drooped. "Point is, they haven't gotten to see you the way I do now: humble, down-to-earth, and willing to give anything and everything for someone you care about. The boys see it!" He looked at me and then back to Sterling's contemplative gaze. "I'd say give it time, except I know some want you to fail; they're just waiting for you to start losing."

9
Sack of Flour

Sterling and Viola Harris welcomed their second child, John, into the world near the end of 1929. He was born on October 29th, Black Tuesday. Joe Rinaldi had made good on his promise, making a name for himself and his family as an All-American, leading Tooele to its first Class A football state championship title, but the news was quickly overshadowed by the town's bank failure: a threat to most everyone's good name. Every day there were new articles about the long reaching effects a stock market crash would have. Still, at the time, no one could fully comprehend the creeping devastation the Great Depression would eventually unravel. Although most of us never thought it would really touch Tooele, a couple years of downcast articles later and it most surely did: slowly, if not quickly, affecting everyone in one way or another. My family sold off everything we could, vacating our home and leaving the gas station desolate. We moved in with Grandma and Grandpa Shields. Dad tried out his hand as a small business owner once again, consolidating a bigger operation into a place for all your household needs, Lacey's Hardware, which also became known as "The Winchester Store." Times were hard, but there was still a need for certain things.

I watched when Skipper took down the newspaper article that read "Tooele Gridders Win Utah Class A Title" and replaced it with "Depression Hits Tooele" on the street boards at the barbershop. Another read "24 Tooele Men Leave for Federal Government Forest Jobs." A few years later, in 1932, several farmers now sat along the streets in their overalls waiting for jobs. One man had his hat over his face and was sleeping against the wall of the barbershop. He awoke when he heard Skipper handling a newspaper. "How much do they pay you to do that, Skipper?" It was Clay's dad.

"I get a nickel a day, after I deliver everyone's paper," Skipper said proudly.

"Do you need help?" Clay's dad asked. The football team was gathered nearby and Clay cowered out of view.

"No, I'll manage. Thanks!" Skipper finished tacking a paper to the board, picked up the remaining papers, and left me standing there reading the new material.

One article was titled, "Tooele Bank Closure Costs Farmers' Land"; another was "International Smelter Forced to Restrict Hours." Sterling walked up from behind me, while I was reading. He posted his own flyer on the news board.

In bold letters at the top it read, "Barn Raising." Then directly under that, it read, "Come hungry. Will feed workers." At the bottom it read, "Where: Sterling's Place," and then on the next line, "When: Saturday."

"Will you bring your parents and come help, Joe?"

"Yeah, of course, Coach."

"I'm getting all the supplies from your dad's place. I think your mom will like what Viola has in mind for our barn—a closer venue for dancing." He laughed.

A large group, including those of us in summer football camp, followed Sterling and Mike Melinkovich into the music shop. People waiting in the street for work curiously observed and then several stood up to see the sign Sterling had posted. Some even lost their place for a handout in the bread line.

"Hurry up, Mike!" Mr. Rinaldi leaned over a crowd of shoulders. "They'll be broadcasting on the hour."

The football team and as many other curious people from town who could squeeze into the music shop, anxiously waited for Mr. Melinkovich to put five cents into the radio box. The coin clanked inside the empty box.

Sterling adjusted the tuner and the volume. "Thousands continue to lose jobs and youth from all over the nation have begun riding the rails and sleeping in hobo jungle camps, in search of a day's wage. In other news, the twenty-first amendment was signed into law and the days of prohibition are officially over."

"How's that?" Sterling asked.

"One more turn," George Sr. said.

Sterling turned the tuning knob a little farther. "That question again for our national audience—what player on the current Notre Dame roster is known as the Tooelee Mink?"

"George Melinkovich!" the current football players yelled excitedly. Mike Melinkovich smiled broadly. "It's not Too-ill-ee. It's Tooele!"

"Here's a hint," the radio announcer continued. "This is a recording of the now famous opening kickoff of Notre Dame's 1931 season." Another voice sounded, "The kick is up. It's a high flyer. Notre Dame receives it at the two." A different voice commented, "Oh, he should have let this one go." The first recorded voice returned. "He's got to run it now. He's already to the twenty. He's got blockers. He slips past a tackler to the thirty. Another tackler misses. He's to the forty. The fifty. He shifts his hips and avoids two more to the other forty now. They might not stop him. He's just got the kicker to beat, and he does—spinning his way to the twenty. The ten. Touchdown! Notre Dame. What a start to the season." The second recorded voice spoke up again. "Notre Dame's freshman return man just scored the first points of the season. Amazing! What was his name?"

The present radio announcer interrupted, "And that is exactly what we are asking you."

"Um, is it Frank Leahy?"

"No, I'm sorry, the return man was Notre Dame's current fullback, George Melinkovich, out of Tooelee, Utah."

"Hooray Tooele!" Our cheers echoed into the street. "Go George!"

"He's really something," Mr. Karabatsos commented and exited.

Others patted Mr. Melinkovich's shoulder on the way out and thanked him for letting them listen in.

"We could sure use him this year," Sterling told George. "We've lost more than we've won."

"Is the principal giving you trouble again, Sterl?" George asked.

"No, I think he and I have an understanding." Sterling held the door as George exited. "But there is always someone who thinks they can do my job better."

Outside the shop a man in dirty overalls confronted Mr. Karabatsos. "Why don't you go back to your country? Give real Americans their jobs back!" He staggered after Mr. Karabatsos and slurred the words he spoke.

Elmer Searle stepped into the man's path. "Dad, you're drunk."

The boys from the team all stood scattered around the spectacle and stared.

"And you, too." Mr. Searle tried to point at Mr. Rinaldi walking by, but his arm flopped back down over his son's shoulder. Elmer caught the weight of his father and held him upright. "Hey, you don't play football no more. What are yuh doin' with them?"

Sterling hurried over and helped Elmer. They each stepped under an arm and walked Mr. Searle to the closest building; they set him up against the wall. Elmer sat down next to him.

"I lost the farm," Mr. Searle blubbered to Elmer. "Only the dagos, wops, and Greeks have jobs now."

"Would you even want to work at the smelter, Elden? You're a pig farmer." Sterling casually sat down on the other side of Mr. Searle, looking in the distance.

"What do you care? All that matters to you are silly football games." Mr. Searle lifted his head and rolled it around on his shoulders until he was looking at Sterling sideways. His eyes were bloodshot and glazed over. "They took the title to my farm."

"The bank won't sell your land. Who on earth could buy it from them, anyway?"

Mr. Searle didn't reply.

Sterling continued, "The bank is not going to make you move until they have a buyer. You raise those pigs and buy your land. It's going to be all right." He looked at the broken man before him, clearly pondering. "Tell you what. You sober up and then you and Elmer come back and see me. I might have some sway with getting a loan until you can get work."

The team had dispersed but Mr. Melinkovich stood waiting for Sterling.

Sterling got up and walked over to Mr. Melinkovich. "It's legal to drink now, but I'm glad I have nothing to do with that stuff. There is no drinking away your problems."

"But you only drank when it's customary," Mr. Melinkovich said.

"Not anymore," Sterling said.

"I wonder what people will make of that?" Mr. Melinkovich asked.

"Whatever they want," Sterling shrugged. "Hmph, like they always do."

"Don't you figure some will be offended?"

"Are you offended?" Sterling put his arm around his friend's shoulders.

Mr. Melinkovich paused and stared past Sterling thoughtfully, and then he looked directly back. He let out a big laugh. "Ha! No, of course not. Why would I ever be offended by you? Takes a bigger man than me, is all, taking a stand like that." Mr. Melinkovich put his arm up on Sterling's shoulders as they walked away.

☙

Where's Coach?" Willis Smith asked Mr. Gowans.

"Have you two seen Coach?" Mr. Gowans turned around and questioned our new ball boys, Dan Gillespie and Bub Bevan, seated in the stands. They shook their heads.

A low buzz circulated through the stands. "There he is," yelled Mr. Rinaldi.

Coach Harris' unmistakable figure emerged in the distance carrying a weight on his shoulder.

Clay, Elmer, and X sat in the stands now as graduates to the program.

"He's late!" Clay sneered. "See, rules still don't apply to him!"

Elmer shoved a hard elbow into Clay's sternum thrusting him backward off the bench and onto the next row.

"What was that for?" Clay laughed. "I was only fooling."

Elmer pointed at the coach. "Family comes before the team." He got to his feet and walked over to help Sterling.

Coach steadily plodded along the stamped down grass path to the playing field. A wave of recognition moved from one end of the crowd to the other, as persons rose to their feet acknowledging their coach with applause, Viola carried over one shoulder like a sack of flour. His two-year-old, John, and his four-year-old, Richard, trailed behind.

"What's wrong with her?" Mr. Mitchell tapped me from behind, in between shelling peanuts near our bench.

"It started with blurred vision soon after John's birth, then it was trouble walking. Coach has taken her to every doctor around, even went to the Mayo Clinic."

"Is she okay?" Elmer asked, with sincere concern.

"She'll be fine. She wanted to come, so I brought her. Doctors even named it this time—multiple sclerosis—though they don't know what that rightly means anymore than you or I do." Sterling adjusted and hoisted John into his other arm. The rest of the team got up to help. "It's okay, just wait there; I'm going to find Viola and the boys a nice seat to watch from, and then we can play some football."

Sterling set Viola next to Mrs. Melinkovich, in the partially integrated crowd. He gently kissed her on the forehead and handed her a blanket. She faintly said, "Food luck." Her mouth formed three more inaudible words—*I love you.*

"How are my boys?" Mike Melinkovich asked Dick and John. John squirmed past Mrs. Melinkovich to see Mr. Melinkovich.

"Oh Chonny, Chonny." Mrs. Melinkovich put a hand on his cheek as he stepped past. "Getting so big now."

Sterling returned to his team. "Who will pray for us?" No one raised a hand. "How about I say this one." He looked into the stands and then bowed and offered a prayer in the huddle of his players.

Skipper busily erased and posted a new score almost as quickly as Granite scored them. At halftime it was 13–0. Sterling gave Mr. Gowans the clipboard. "I'll be back." Sterling checked on his wife and decided to carry her home. Mrs. Melinkovich and the kids followed. He did not return until the final quarter. Then he exchanged words with a flustered assistant and failed to console him. Mr. Gowans gave back the clipboard and walked off.

The final was Granite Farmers 20, Tooele Tigers 0.

Mr. Mitchell threw his bag of peanut shells on the ground.

☙

Several women from church were inside Sterling's home when he and I entered the door. Sterling removed his hat. "What is all this?"

"We brought you dinner." Mrs. Smith twisted a cap onto a jar she had just canned with food and placed it on the counter among other filled jars. She turned her gaze to the table filled with soups, salads, and casseroles.

"Where's Mrs. Melinkovich?"

"Oh, we didn't need her help anymore. We sent her home." Mrs. Mills dried a plate in her hands with a towel. "Mrs. Hanks is in the bedroom attending to Viola."

Sterling gawked, speechless.

Mrs. Whitehouse stopped feather dusting and took the hands of the two boys. "I'll get these guys cleaned up and fed."

"Why did you send her home? Did you ask her if she wanted to help?" he asked.

"We couldn't understand her English," Mrs. Mills said.

"She comes here nearly every day and she helps us, not just once in a while, but every day. We've paid her to be our house help the last two years. What's to understand?"

The women's eyes widened and looked away; they kept working at their tasks.

Sterling clenched his teeth, didn't say anything more, and walked past them into Viola's room.

Mrs. Hanks sat in a chair at Viola's bedside. She held out a spoonful of split pea and bacon soup and gently held it to Viola's mouth.

Viola smiled at Sterling "The sisters have been taking good care of me."

Sterling smiled. "May I speak with my wife?"

Mrs. Hanks walked out of the open door. I stood waiting in the passageway.

Sterling stepped close to the bedside. "They sent Mrs. Melinkovich home."

"Oh, they mean well, Sterl. Give them a break!" Viola rubbed Sterling's arm at the bedside. "Mrs. Melinkovich needed a break, anyway."

"They don't even know her." Sterling looked away, disgusted.

Viola tried to cover it up, but she started laughing uncontrollably, shaking even.

"What's so funny?" Sterling asked.

She tried to explain but only more laughter came. She doubled up on the bed laughing into her covers.

"What is it?" Sterling looked at me. "What did I say?"

I shrugged.

"Don't you see? You have been trying like mad to get this town to help others, and now when they finally do—they can't do it to your liking." Viola laughed again.

Sterl threw her hand back to her. He threw his own hands up in the air.

"It hurts to laugh, but I needed it. I haven't laughed like that in a while," she said.

Sterl took her hand, again. "Well, don't strain yourself."

"Promise me you will thank the Relief Society women for what they have done here." Viola held Sterling's hand with both of hers and looked lovingly in his eyes.

Sterling nodded slowly. "I promise!"

10

A Vested Community

In 1933, Sterling changed tactics. Whether winning or not on the field, losing his community was a more bleak possibility. He asked to be on the agenda for the next Tooele City Council meeting that was open to the public. He invited the representatives of the International Smelter, members of the school board, Elmer Searle, Tom Greene of the Tooele Mercantile Company, and me.

"What's your young friend doing here?" the president of the City Council asked.

"He'll be our next All-American. With his lead, we will win another state championship: only this time with defense. With your approval, we'd like to represent any company in town who would like to sponsor us: at a minimum marketing fee, of course. If we go to state, that kind of publicity will be more than worth it," Sterling said confidently.

"And if you don't? You can't guarantee state! I hate to say it, but you've been quite average the last few years." He scoffed.

"Then I will resign as football coach," Sterling said. "You have my word."

The people in attendance gasped. Eyes darted around but no one objected.

"It's a win-win," Sterling proclaimed. "Either way, the team gets uniforms it desperately needs, and if we get excess support, the money goes back to the community."

"You have a flare for the dramatic, Mr. Harris." The president paused. "So you're saying you're not afraid of losing your coaching income?" he mused.

"I want to see this community succeed at all cost. I'm willing to lay it all out there." Sterling stood poised, hands clasped behind his back.

"How do you propose to gather and distribute these monies?" the president asked.

"Sponsors may sign up at my barn-raising event. I suggest the community forms an unemployment line to give out loans for those between work. I'd also like to ask if it is permissible for me to hold livestock for folks like Mr. Searle to work out of my barn? In the shade and out of any dust bowl effect."

"It's your personal property. It's zoned for more than your horses, should you please. I don't see any reason Mr. Searle could not work there under his work permit." The president looked at the rest of the board for consent. Each nodded agreement. "Tell me more about your idea for this unemployment line."

Sterling looked at Mr. Melinkovich. "I will speak to that," Mike responded. "The International Smelter is currently working with stores and shops to provide credit for laid-off workers. The company will pay the tab for commodities determined essential to each home, month to month. Upon return to employment, these loans must be paid back, but overtime will be available. This has worked for us. Since Sterling is friends with many of the Smelter workers, as citizens we would like to make a donation to set up a similar program and fund projects for city workers."

C. R. McBride spoke up. "The Tooele Valley Railway would be interested in matching those funds. I would be happy to personally facilitate the program if you need an office wing to distribute unemployment loans."

"We've been needing to build roads from Tooele to Bingham," the President said.

"Coach Harris, in exchange for sponsorship, I could donate all of the uniforms and equipment you need. Can you make my signage bigger than the railway and the smelter?" Mr. Greene added. Everyone laughed.

"It looks like you have everyone in agreement. Motion to proceed." The President looked at the other members. One seconded the motion and all hands raised unanimously.

☙

A buzz of life circulated through the town. Most hoped upon hope without much else to believe in when reduced to taking handouts. Some suspected it was even more impossible for a small town like Tooele to break through for a second outright state championship. Surely the state of Utah could see the injustice and not let it happen to the same team twice. A few felt Sterling was just stubborn enough to pull it off though, against all odds. Even the doubters would not bet against him. They chipped in as well. I was determined to do my part and stack those odds back in our favor with all I had. I gave it my all in that very first game of the year. But then came a huge blow. It would become common practice for Sterling to bring the football results to my bedside. He slapped down the paper with the first results. "They say you were a terror out there. They think we won't win another game without our defensive captain."

Near the end of the first game, the referee treated a gash in my forehead with unwashed hands and I contracted scarlet fever carried from his treatment of a neighboring town. Just like that, it looked like we were down and out.

The band burst into music outside my home, playing our fight song. Sterling watched from the window, by the quarantined sign. A tear came down his cheek. "What the paper doesn't know is we have already won!" he proclaimed. "Have you ever seen anything like it?" I crept to my feet and peered out the window. There was everyone I knew at school in Oldtown and Newtown cheering, "Fight, fight, fight!" Even the clouds of the sky parted with glorious rays of light. The town closed up shop during football games, from then on, home or away. The football team didn't disappoint either. There was no explanation for it other than a united cause and sheer grit. The team was ferocious in extending our season to the final game, as promised—the state championship—long enough to make my return. That game was against none other than Box Elder. They were determined to prove we didn't belong. But we beat them 20–6.

☙

The band marched in front of a black truck with wood boards caging the back portion as it drove up to the Town Hall where I waited with the team. Banners were draped that read: *1933 State Champs*.

"Where did you get the truck?" Kenneth Shields asked Sterling when he stepped out of the passenger-side.

"We're borrowing it," Sterling said.

"From who?" Joe Rinaldi questioned.

"Principal Mills." Sterling looked back at the truck and Principal Mills stepped out from the driver's side. The team players exchanged looks of surprise. Viola stayed in the truck.

More black trucks pulled up, most with sponsoring banners attached to the side, each representing a different town store.

"Load up, gents." Sterling walked to the driver's side of the truck he had come in.

"There hasn't been an automobile on these streets for years." Wayne paused before climbing into the back of a truck.

I stretched a hand down to him. "There hasn't been anything to celebrate for a while, either," I said.

The first team's offense and defense loaded the first four trucks and the rest of us piled in to the remaining black trucks. Sterling drove the first truck with Viola in the passenger seat. Superintendent Nielsen drove the next truck with Principal Mills climbing into the passenger seat. And storeowners and managers followed after that.

The trucks entered East Street and honked their horns for those waiting—a good mixture of Oldtown fans and Newtown fans on each side of the street. The people waved and shouted, throwing their hats in the air as we passed by. Closed signs swung in the wind against the glass doors of shops. The parade turned back onto Main Street and the trucks drove to the theater and parked there in a semicircle, forming a backdrop. The sign above the theater advertised the movie *Wild Boys, Teenagers Riding the Rails.*

Principal Mills stood in the middle facing the people who gathered. Gerald Gillespie walked up and whispered something in Principal Mills's ear, to which he nodded. He waited until everyone was ready and they quit chattering.

"As Principal of Tooele High School, I proudly present Coach Harris with this placard honoring his team as the 1933 Class A football champions of the state of Utah."

Principal Mills shook Sterling's hand and gave him the placard. "Congratulations," he mouthed, not audible over the cheers. "Now the Champions of 1933 have something to give to Mr. Harris."

Gerald and I carried the team's water barrel, filled to the brim with grass instead, and placed it at Sterling's feet. "This is for next season, when you get nervous and need something to chew on," Kenneth Shields laughed.

"Whose idea was this?" Sterling laughed. "Let me guess." He looked at Gerald.

"Gerald's," Kenneth said.

"Thanks, Goof. Many of your boys have come home with one of my nicknames—Guts Shields, Danny Savage, Swilly Searle—and you can see why this one is Goof Gillespie. We're going to miss you, goof." Sterling placed a hand on Gerald's shoulder. "We are going to miss all of the seniors." The crowd clapped briefly, but Sterling interrupted, "We all have been through hard times, but this group refused to give in."

The crowd applauded.

"Joe, we couldn't have won this championship without your minutes. I'm glad you were healthy enough to play in the final game."

Again the crowd cheered and applauded.

"Jim Rinaldi, we're going to need another quarterback who can run that spinner out of the punt formation."

Everyone cheered and clapped.

"We have been called by many names over the years—Tigers, Smelterites, a few unmentionable, and Champions." The crowd interrupted him with cheers or laughs for each designation. "But, I have never been more proud than when I saw another headline in the paper that called us Sterling's Men." The crowd erupted. "These boys are fine men and I have appreciated my time with them. I also have an announcement. I won't be back next season."

Everyone went silent.

"I need to spend more time with my wife and kids. Mike Melinkovich has a position in the personnel department at the Smelter lined up for me. I'll be able to work a little among friends and, when needed, I'll be able to be home with my wife.

"I'm going to miss coaching. I'm going to miss our fans. Thank you!"

Sterling walked over to the truck he had driven. He opened the passenger side and hefted Viola over his shoulder. The crowd parted, one town of fans. We clapped quietly as he walked through and then stood in silence, in awe, and watched him walk off into the sunset, away from football for the last time. The crowd converged again and hoisted the seniors onto their shoulders, cheering and carrying on. I gave one last look in the direction of Sterling's silhouette and then looked at the community that embraced me.

It would take several years to realize the full impact of what Sterling had done for our community, but many of us knew full well his influence in our individual lives never could and never would fully be measured in this life.

Epilogue
Legacy, in a Name

Years later, in 1940, I entered my old high school. An older Sterling Harris opened the door of an office to let the stake president, Loren C. Dunn, out. President Dunn was dressed in a nice suit and tie. I stood, a grown man now, waiting for him in the hall. President Dunn shook Sterling's hand. "There's a saying that says if you want something done, ask a busy man to do it. Pray about it with your wife."

"Well, hello Mr. Lacey." President Dunn shook my hand heartily. "I've heard some good news about you. Is it true?"

"Yes, it is."

"Well, congratulations." President Dunn went on his way.

Sterling took me by the hand. We entered his office and sat down. On his desk was his nameplate—Superintendent Harris. "It's good to see you, Joe."

"I like your office."

"Yeah, eleven years going. Viola won't let me leave; she thinks the students of this town still need me. She never worries about herself."

"How is she doing?" I asked. "I'd like to see her."

"Her multiple sclerosis keeps her from moving much now. She has really hung in there, though. She's on oxygen tanks, but she accepts visitors."

"I heard they are naming the new elementary school in your name," I said.

"Oh, yeah, they are making a big deal out of nothing, if you ask me." Sterling waved a hand, shrugging the honor off.

"Well, if you ask me, it's not sufficient for all you have done," I said.

"So what brings you here, Joe? What's new in your life?"

"Mary Whitehouse has accepted my proposal. I'm getting married!"

Sterling got a look in his eye. "Oh, I see. After all this time, don't tell me you're going to up and become Mormon for a pretty girl, are you?"

"Oh no, I'm not saying I'm getting baptized." I shrugged.

"Oh, forgive me." Sterling shifted in his chair. "I was thinking you were here to make good on that deal you pitched me some time back, you know, to have me perform your baptism."

"Well, President Dunn doesn't just visit anyone. Not to be presumptuous, but it sounded to me like you're the next bishop."

"Now, now, I haven't given him an answer, yet, Joe."

"Well, I hope your first ordinance as a bishop is performing my marriage to Mary."

"That would be an honor," Sterling said. "If you have time, maybe you can come by the house with me."

ଓ

Rocko stood corralled at Sterling's house. "Rocko is still a beautiful horse," I said. "Do you still ride him?"

"Of course. Every day. I ride up Middle Canyon." He pointed toward the canyon. "Up there is a mountain bench. You can see the entire valley and the Great Salt Lake."

We walked into the house and into Viola's room. She smiled. "I know who this young man is." Her voice resonated into the plastic oxygen mask over her mouth.

"Hi, Viola. You look beautiful."

Viola laughed. "No, I don't, but I used to get dressed up and look nice—to dance."

"I remember," I told her.

"It's you who looks brighter, Joe. Something about you has changed. You look very happy."

"He has good news." Sterling put an arm around my shoulders.

"I'm getting married to my sweetheart."

Tears flooded Viola's cheeks. She smiled happily. Silently.

"I'm hoping Sterl will oversee the wedding." I looked at Sterling.

"I have some news as well," Sterling told Viola. "Brother Dunn approached me about becoming the bishop."

Viola weakly wiped her face dry. "And what did you say?"

"I told him I don't have time, of course, and what little time I do have I want to spend with you." Sterling got to his knees next to her bedside and took her hand in his.

"Sterl, my love, you were there for the youth of this town when they needed you. You were there for the Smelter workers when they needed you. You returned to the school when the town realized how much they needed you for their children." Sterling lowered his head into the bed at her side and tears came. "The Lord knows who he needs to preside over this town now," Viola put her hand on Sterling's head.

Sterling raised his head after a while. "And if I'm not worthy?"

"Oh you." She swatted at him with her free hand. "What are you worried about? You have done nothing the Lord cannot forgive you for. He knows who he has called to this work. Be there for Him!"

Sterling performed the civil marriage between Mary and me, and he served as a bishop for many faithful years.

☙

Back in 1992, standing before the congregation of admirers all brought together by, and in behalf of, the man before me in the closed casket, a mentor and second father to many of us. I cleared my throat and spoke again. "Some may wonder why I have been one so honored to represent the hundreds of men and women whose lives have been touched by Sterling R. Harris. It comes by assignment. Back in 1985 when we lived in California, we were completing our annual visit to Tooele. Before heading home, we made an early morning visit to say goodbye to Coach and Neva." Yes, Coach was blessed with another wife, late in life. "Coach's legs were horribly swollen and he was feeling rotten. We both sensed that this would be the last goodbye as he was leaving to go to the LDS hospital that morning. As the ambulance pulled up, Coach said 'Joe, I want you to speak at my funeral.' It came as a shock, and the thought crossed my mind that he was delirious or disoriented." Some of the people in attendance giggled.

"However, it was not the last goodbye, and thanks to Neva, Dr. Jim Orme (a former football player of Sterling's), caring sons, countless friends, and his love of life, he fought back—enduring with dignity to the end, and then finally temporal death, the death to the body, took over.

"John Harris, of significant age himself, held his father's hand in his own.

Sterling sang softly in a raspy voice, 'Here's a Tiger in Tooeleee.' Sterling coughed a few times. He spoke the words now, 'Three cheers in a Tiger.' He coughed. 'Rah, rah, rah, yeah,' he stopped. 'If

I could just have one more ride on old Rocko,' were his last audible words to John," I told the congregation.

"Though my eyes are misty and my words come hard, it is fitting to remind ourselves that this service should be regarded as a celebration, for aging and death is part of God's plan for His family to learn, but also to return to Him. Who can say positively that Sterling is not looking down in his spirit form and listening to this heartfelt tribute? I think he would smile to see all of us together, a community united like family. In Jesus's name, Amen." I sat down behind Bishop Bevan.

Joel Dunn took my place at the podium and began speaking. Bishop Bevan shook my hand and thanked me for my words, as did his counselors.

"Most of us don't understand people like Sterling. There is a certain caliber of people sent to Earth for specific reasons. Those reasons are too complicated for most of us to understand."

I nodded my head in agreement. Soon Joel finished his talk in the name of Jesus Christ and returned to a seat with the congregation next to his dark-complexioned wife.

Elder Loren C. Dunn took his place and spoke briefly too.

"I bring the best wishes, concern, and love from the Church's First Presidency to the Harris family. I had the privilege of growing up in the same neighborhood and having a close association with the Harris family. Sterling has had a peaceable walk in the community. He brought peace and good and light to the community. Sterling left a legacy of brotherhood and accomplishments. Those accomplishments will survive future generations. I remember the day we dedicated Sterling Harris Elementary. People of all complexions stood together wholly integrated and sang the opening song, 'America the Beautiful,' with the newly raised American flag flying overhead. Sterling got the rare pleasure that day to see while yet in life, his accomplishment of uniting us. We must not make him out to be some kind of perfect 'saint,' but we will always remember him for the nickname that has become his—Bridge Builder. In the name of Jesus Christ, Amen."

Notes

Sterling led Tooele to be State Champs in 1928, '29, and '33, winning 80 percent of the time, with a win-loss record of 58–14–3.

The 1929 Tooele State Champs share the record of most shutouts in a season to this day (10).

One of Sterling's players, Dan Gillespie, coached Tooele to become State Champs in 1937.

It took Tooele sixty-five years to earn the title of State Champs again, in 2002, but at the 3A level designation.

Tooele beat Judge Memorial 157–0.

Sterling Harris served as personnel director at the smelter for many years, ensuring "his boys" had summer jobs to allow them to go to college.

Sterling Harris served as Superintendent of the Tooele County School district for twenty-five years.

Sterling Harris Elementary School is a monument dedicated to his name that stands today on East Street (the former border to a once-divided town).

Sterling Harris became bishop of the Tooele community in 1951.

Joe Lacey went on to play college football for the Utah State Aggies. Several boys played college ball at places like the University of Utah, BYU, and Notre Dame.

Colonel (Ret.) Peter Joseph Lacey, Jr. served for thirty years in various roles in the army. Several boys gave military service, many served missions, and many became doctors, lawyers, and other highly respected professionals in their communities.

Joe Lacey proposed to and married his childhood sweetheart, Mary Whitehouse, in 1940, though "with tears" she lamented how she always thought she would marry in the temple.

Joe Lacey was baptized a member of The Church of Jesus Christ of Latter-day Saints in 1943 while preparing for World War II. He said it was "long overdue," but with the thought of possibly dying, he decided it was time.

Peter Joseph Lacey, Jr. and Mary Whitehouse were later married for time and all eternity in the Logan Utah Temple.

Joe Lacey was able to serve faithfully in many church callings, including bishop.

References

Blanthorn, Ouida, comp. *A History of Tooele County*. Centennial County History Series, 1998. Accessed September 4, 2015, http://utahhistory.sdlhost.com/#/item/000000011019561.

Dunn, Loren C. "Before I Build a Wall," *Ensign*, May 1991.

"Death: Sterling R. Harris. *Deseret News*, Sept. 15, 1992. http://www.deseretnews.com/article/247625/DEATH--STERLING-R-HARRIS.html?pg=all.

Interviews with Don Norton. English Department, Brigham Young University.

"John Sterling Harris." *Daily Herald*, Sept. 29, 2013. http://www.heraldextra.com/lifestyles/announcements/obituaries/john-sterling-harris/article_cf6accd7-2ec9-50c9-8c35-11ec4822f184.html.

Lacey, Peter Joseph. *Personal History of Colonel Joe Lacey (U.S. Army, retired)*. Salt Lake City, UT: P. J. Lacey, 1998.

"Obituary: Peter Joseph Lacey Jr." *Deseret News*, May 9, 2006. http://www.deseretnews.com/article/1057414/Obituary-Peter-Joseph-Lacey-Jr.html?pg=all.

Salt Lake Tribune. 1929, microfilm.

The Tooele Transcript Bulletin. Feb. 1928–Dec. 1936, microfilm.

"Utah High School Activities Association Sports Records Book." UHSAA. Accessed September 4, 2015, www.uhsaa.org/RecordsBook/Records_BookFootball.pdf

A portrait of Sterling Harris, ca. 1954, currently hanging in Sterling Harris Elementary. Photo courtesy of Marianne Hollien.

The 1929 Tooele High School championship football team.

Acknowledgments

I will not be able to thank everyone specifically who has helped me along the way, mostly by way of encouragement through all of these years of pursuing the writing dream. I appreciate my wife's patience, love, and support as I give so much time and energy to my love of writing. Of course, I must thank my family, especially my parents, Ray and Robyn Parker, my friends, and my colleagues for reading, editing, and most of all for listening to me bounce ideas off them, even when it likely sounded more like complaining. I often felt overwhelmed and stuck in the quagmire of problematic prose through years and years of rewrites and revisions. But my friends and family lifted my sights to keep after my highest aspirations and goals. Most will never know what difficult times and challenges had to be faced and overcome for this work to come to be.

I am thankful to writers groups, classmates, and a professor of philosophy and film (art and literature) at BYU named Dennis Packard who never gave up on the project and its possibilities. I also must tip my hat to Don Norton, an emeritus English professor from BYU, who originally saw the potential in his family history research. He and his students conducted interviews and transcribed oral histories of persons who were profoundly affected by Sterling Harris's life, during the football years in particular. I, myself, was able to sit down with his son John Sterling Harris on occasion, while he was yet alive, and talk about anything under the sun, including a lot of context for depicting this key portion of his father's life.

I am grateful to the editors, graphic artists, authors, marketers, publishers, and others who helped with the business aspects and questions that invariably arise in making publication a reality.

About the Author

CHAD ROBERT PARKER lived in six states growing up and is the second of six boys. Each served a two-year mission. He is the son of two great, humble parents. They taught him a love for family, church, and life. Chad is an avid sports fan and likes creating games. He also likes juggling: he chose to juggle publishing his first book with getting married and starting a new venture hosting Anecdoting.com, a site to share and collect good everyday life stories. Chad works in the library at BYU and lives in beautiful Saratoga Springs, Utah, with his lovely wife.

For more information and news,
visit www.chadrobertparker.com
or scan the QR code provided here.

0 26575 17352 9